About the author

Keshav Aneel is a much loved author of two books. His works *Promise Me a Million Times* and *The One From The Stars* are national bestsellers, and have received praises for the spiritual essence and life lessons they carried. The latter work was also upheld for very sensitively highlighting struggles of a child born in a middle class family, with many of them forcing their parents to read. Apart from writing, Keshav is a motivational speaker and a poet, and runs a Youtube channel.

Keshav Aneel.

Our Story of Love

KESHAV ANEEL

Srishti
PUBLISHERS & DISTRIBUTORS

SRISHTI PUBLISHERS & DISTRIBUTORS
Registered Office: N-16, C.R. Park
New Delhi – 110 019
Corporate Office: 212A, Peacock Lane
Shahpur Jat, New Delhi – 110 049
editorial@srishtipublishers.com

First published by
Srishti Publishers & Distributors in 2019

10 9 8 7 6 5 4 3 2 1

When you are 26, your parents expect you to settle in a job, earn well and get married at the soonest. They very idea of doing something unconventional is bound to irritate them, and they would only be disappointed.

However, I am blessed with the most different mother and father. They told me to just be happy. To enjoy my time, and be honest with my own self. They showed faith in what I wanted to achieve, and allowed me to chase my dreams.

This book, or my writing career, wouldn't have been possible without their belief in me. I want to tell them that I love them, and want to see them the proudest of me.

Acknowledgements

I would like to thank team Srishti Publishers, especially Mr Jayanta Kumar Bose and Arup Bose, for their relentless support. They have always made themselves available to my ideas, and have helped in their potential best to build my career. Every time I have given them a call, they have obliged with help, and never said no to whatever could be done to make my work reach readers.

Stuti – my editor at Srishti, thank you so much for taking care of the mess that I create with words. Your presence makes my journey so smooth and stress free.

Merril Anil, like always, remains to be the most amazing person I have ever met. Thank you for designing a beautiful cover, giving your honest feedback on the stories I keep writing, and being there for me. I know, even if it's for the

Acknowledgements

hundredth time in a day I am calling you, you will only smile and assist me.

Pankaj Giri – We don't talk much on phone because both of us are so busy nowadays. But brother, I'll never forget the low time when I wasn't getting published; you were the one who motivated me and gave me hope. Brother, I love you and I wish I could explain in words what you mean to me.

Likhit Avasthi! You are the man I want to be like. Thank you for all the spiritual lessons. For all your endeavours in making me a better human being. You are my dark knight. My personal Batman.

The Sylvester Stallone story that motivates the protagonist in this book was taken from the logicalindian.com. So, I would like to thank them too. They have put it there in an exceptionally beautiful manner.

Prologue

I cannot remember the number of times I have done this in the past – sit and just look at my wife. She is on the other side of the room, shuttling between the bed and the wooden wardrobe, arranging her clothes. Every time her eyes meet mine, she passes a gentle smile. I can see how strongly she is trying to hold herself, to deviate her mind and show me that she is not hurt. Maybe she thinks, speaking of pain that shall never subside only ends up making others feel equally depressed.

But honestly, I don't want this! This overflowing sense of maturity in her. She must not bury her feelings inside her heart and live unheard, that's all I know. I want her to talk, to fight, to cry, to share, to let it out of her system, but then, this is how she has always been. She seldom mentions her pain, because she knows it bothers me more.

Prologue

In all these years of togetherness, and all the mad ups and downs we have faced to be with each other, there hasn't been a fraction of a second when my care for her has dwindled a bit. And she knows what that eventually always leads to. The moment I see her in tears, I'll not hesitate to implement any wise, or even foolish idea, to make her forget all her problems.

I understand how broken she feels right now. My eyes well up wondering what wrong she has done to be handed this life-long suffering. To see nature depriving her of what she deserves and so madly desires, is burning me from deep within.

A few moments ago, we learnt through a medical report that she won't ever be able to conceive. I realize she is devastated and that she is waiting for me to get here and there, so that she can lock herself in the washroom and cry her eyes out. However, today, like every other day since we have met, I won't let that happen. If she is breaking into tears, it has to happen in my arms.

I can't take her silence anymore and stand up to walk towards her. She remains engrossed in her chore, while I gaze at her, waiting for her to stop and notice. She slows down, knowing that I am right behind her, but ignores me.

I know what she needs right now. I reach out to her hand, inch closer towards her and lovingly turn her face towards me. Without a word, I hold her in an embrace as soft as a feather, yet as firm as a mountain.

Prologue

After some initial resistance, when I don't let her go, she finally gives in and locks her arms around me, burying her face in my chest. It seems she was desperately wanting and waiting for it. I rest my chin on her head for a few seconds. Then, I softly kiss it.

Talking about our children and joking that I would tell all her stories to them had been my way of calming her down on rough days. On every mention of having kids, she would brim with brightness, chattering away. I had always seen her phone gallery flooded with pictures and videos of little kids showing off their adorable idiosyncrasies. She always felt so excited and happy seeing all that, thinking, one day she would have her own child doing all those cute things. Since we had gotten along, it was her number one dream, to be a mother. To have a child... who looked exactly like both of us.

It wasn't an extraordinary wish, I guess. Almost every woman dreams of it, and is granted. Then why did she have to suffer? I feel sorry, hugging her tighter. Nobody, no matter who they are, deserves to be tricked out of the simplest gifts of life. The proudest thing about being a girl is that she has the power to take this world forward. It's a gift, and it remains her pride for as long as she lives. But, when you take this gift away, it is more a sense of hollowness within, than how the world looks at it.

If there was anything in the world I could do to make my girl smile, make her do away with all her pains and problems,

I would make the stars and the moon dance for her every night.

"You remember you used to say I will always be your first child?" I say. "Huh, darling? You remember that?"

She is quiet. I bend down a bit and plant a peck on her cheek.

"Remember, or you forgot?" I ask.

No answer again. She is unmoved.

"We will always be enough for each other, honey. I promise," I say.

She breathes heavily, looks into my eyes finally, and says in a very soft voice, quivering, "I am not holding you because I am unable to handle this revelation. I am holding you because you have to suffer because of me. And I am scared now."

Insecurities seem to loom high in her mind.

"Been twelve years since we met. I don't think I have loved anything else so much without conditions." I want to reassure her.

"I know that. But I feel... I feel I don't deserve your love anymore."

I react to her invalid sense of guilt rather strongly. I push her slightly away, looking at her in the eyes very sternly, "What are you saying! Had I been in your place, should I have felt this way and left?"

A brief silence follows. I wait for her to answer.

I explain, "Your value doesn't diminish because we can't have something together. You are wrong if you..."

She interrupts, "But not having a child… that's not okay with anyone."

"Who on earth said that?" I say.

'I need to make her laugh or her questions are going to kill her,' I thought.

"Let's do this!" I propose out of nowhere. "Consider me your daughter and dress me up the way you'd want to."

She doesn't reply, considering it a joke. She smiles, and puts it off.

"In fact, that's a brilliant idea. We are doing this!" I say firmly.

"Your mother is going to screw me even if I think about it."

"She won't ever know. I am getting you the makeup kit, wait!"

"Paarth no! I thought that was a joke," she calls out.

I ignore her as I rush to the dressing table, pulling the drawer out and grabbing the box.

"Here it is!" I put it on her hand, and drag her to the sofa.

"Let's do this!" I tell her.

"Please," she almost begs. "This isn't required. I'll be fine."

When my expression does not change, and I keep sitting waiting for her to start, Upasna gives in. She adjusts one knee on the sofa and picks the bottle of moisturizer out of the box.

"I am still saying this isn't required," she warns for the last time.

I point at my face with the thumb.

She gives a freakish smile, squeezing and burying her lips in her mouth. It seems sadistic!

"What is this smile supposed to mean?" I ask, feeling intimidated.

"You will know in a few minutes," she says.

She starts her art work, rubbing the cream between her hands. It is then put around my face. Around the eyes, across the forehead, the nose, the neck, using soft sweeping motions.

Every goat feels the same level of goodness before it is slaughtered, my mind tells me.

As soon as my face is moisturized, she applies something called primer.

"I feel like a drawing sheet to a notorious kid with all intentions to demolish its dignity," I comment.

She ignores my words, and rubs foundation on my face next. She works it in small circular motions using a brush, outwards from the center of my face and down. She does that for about two minutes.

"Let's contour your face now," she mutters.

"Let's what the fuck my face now?" I react. "Haven't you done enough already?"

"We need to define certain parts of it to make you look sexier."

"I hope you are not going to make me wear a bikini next and ask me to dance on a Bhojpuri song for you."

She beams at the idea and I regret uttering it. But she quickly puts something under my eyes, making triangular slopes. She applies the same thing under my nose and then the chin, then the bridge of my nose. She taps it on my skin with a soft sponge like thing. She puts matte powder on the area below my cheekbones, starting from ears to the middle of my cheeks. My forehead is also unable to escape this onslaught.

"Let's take your makeup game to another level." She scares the shit out of me.

Beginning to apply a dark colour on my eyelid with a flat brush, she quickly shifts her concentration on the crease area. In a minute, she finishes it, and going by the trend, I am pretty much sure it's not done yet.

"Now we shall rim your eyes with kohl."

"I was expecting something as meaningless as that."

Upasna uses a kohl pencil on my lower and upper lash line. Now, just when I think the horror is over, the worst part comes. From the washroom, she fetches a Parachute Oil bottle and pours it on her hand, putting its all over my hair. Slowly, I realize, I am given two ponies on my head. I see her pulling an important weapon from her armory – a dark red lipstick! She puts it on the cupid bow of my lips first. I sort of feel as if my gender change operation is getting final touches.

Doing that, she walks three steps back and looks at me, controlling her laughter.

"Something is missing!"

"Now what's left?"

Without saying a word, she goes to the cupboard and pulls a short black-bodycon backless dress.

"This!" she says, pointing at it.

I nearly have a heart attack.

Five minutes later, I stand wearing that sultry piece of cloth. Really tight on the upper part of the torso, it is almost about to come apart from a little above my crotch area. As I step out of the dressing room, saving my respect, covering my chest with both the hands, Upasna breaks into a laugh riot. I am literally feeling naked; I growl. With all my body hair making me look like a wooly mammoth, I stand in one corner of the room, banging my head in the wall, wondering '*Pyar hume kis mod pe le aaya.*'

Controlling herself, she says, "You look like an aged warrior, ready for a tough battle."

'Yeah, with my underwear visible, the enemy is going to run fearing my soldier,' I think.

"If my mother sees what you have done to her son, she will throw you out of the house,' I say.

Upasna comes to hug me, offering some consolation. But instead, she adjusts my side chest fat back in the dress, and brings my hands together, looking at my cleavage. She laughs her heart out, clapping. Then, out of nowhere, she raises her hands and rubs them all over my face. The entire makeup spreads. The little dignity left has gone as well. She drags me to the mirror and grabs her phone from the bed.

"Not a selfie, not a selfie," I shout, jumping away.

She extends her hand, requesting, "Honey please, this shall always stay private."

"Not a chance! This is not a memory; this is humiliation. Utter humiliation," I scream, running around the room.

Nevertheless, she catches me, and drags me to the mirror finally. She moves her hand behind my back, keeping the side of her face on my chest. She adjusts the position of the camera for a full body selfie.

Meanwhile, I look at her, lost, forgetting how I was going to look in the picture. Her goofy smile, the innocence on her face, those large twinkling eyes were such a reason to neglect everything else. She is my most gratifying engagement, and I must take care of her, always.

Together, we have been able to nurture an astonishing connection. Its purity, I can happily say, is felt by everyone who has known our story. We have been an example in our family. We have been an example for our friends. We have been an example for people to understand that love isn't about giving or receiving; it's about having a hope in each other… that you don't let die.

It has been twelve years, mind you. Twelve long years with each other. But when I look back, it only sounds like a thing from yesterday. A thing from just a few hours back.

Twelve Years Ago

It was a hot summer night. I had turned eighteen a few days back. Now I know that's not a big deal, but since childhood, this was the day I had most anxiously waited for. Don't be misguided by American TV shows and movies and think I had decided to lose my virginity or convinced my girlfriend for sex (though I wouldn't have said no to the idea). Just that I had seen my father driving his taxi all through my life, and the yearning to steer around the country like him – which was my second favourite thing to do – had been bubbling inside me.

Surprisingly, I didn't have to learn to drive from anyone; nor would I claim that it was in my blood. Most certainly, I think, it happened because I was interested in it all along. For every single time I had the opportunity, I very keenly observed my father driving, picking up the small nuances of the art while others enjoyed the ride.

However, I wasn't wholly convinced I could handle a car without being formally trained until my old man suffered a paralysis attack. My mother out for some work, my father and I were watching an India-Pakistan cricket match. He, unexpectedly, felt a severe pain on one side of his face, with weakness in his arm. I rushed to help, and noticed he was largely immobile. Terrified, I had no clue what to do. Therefore, I put him in the car, and drove quickly to the nearest hospital. Though we got him medical help well in time, he could no longer function independently. Sadly, he was confined to bed for the rest of his life.

The after effects of the paralysis attack left our family in a financial crunch. We did try looking for different alternatives in terms of anything and everything to earn, but nothing worked in our favour. But now that I had turned 18 and was legal to drive, I was sure bad days were a thing of the past.

I was sitting inside my Toyota Innova in the parking of Indira Gandhi International Airport, Terminal 3. The door on the driving side was half open for ventilation. I lay on the seat that I had reclined back, while my feet rested on the steering wheel. A Kishore Kumar song from the late 70s played on the radio at a very low volume.

I was waiting for someone called Upasna Sharma, coming from Germany. Her flight was supposed to land at around 2:00 a.m. I had come all the way from Chandigarh up to Delhi to pick her up. Since I was going to drive for five hours straight on our way back with this old-sounding lady, I tried getting some sleep. However, I could only manage smiles at my brand new driving license and the writing pad kept on the passenger seat.

What heaven I was experiencing! Finally doing both the things that I earnestly always wished to. Quite obviously, given my appetite for knowledge, I was sad on dropping out of school, but I had no other option. Our savings were almost exhausted and we still needed a whole lot for regular medication for my father.

With that being said, I hope I did not forget to mention my number-one favourite thing. It was writing, and I had the desire that my work be read by people across the world. I was fascinated with the idea ever since I was a child, and I, through my hard work, was consistently making sure I performed my part so that one day I could fulfill this dream.

Despite having studied in a government school, where the medium of communication was Punjabi, my English was good. I had worked very hard on gaining command over the language and would miss no English class ever. I read anything I came across in English – newspapers, pamphlets, advertisements, and even books with the local *raddiwala*. Since I had nobody to practice it with (my friends were least interested and mostly terrible at it), I used to speak in English to myself. I talked to the mirror and watched sports like cricket, football (including the highlights, despite being completely uninterested), WWE and Hollywood movies to understand it better.

My dreams were bigger than the rest of my friends'. Perhaps so big that I wasn't yet granted even a bit of it. *A taxi driver turns into a successful writer and buys a fleet of cars for his company.* I was almost imagining it like a headline. It brought a smile to my face, thinking of the time when all that would finally come true. People asking for autographs, my becoming a celebrity, and the money, of course, giving us all a better life.

The sensation of bugs crawling beneath the skin of my sole brought me back to reality. I put my feet down from the steering and adjusted my chair back in its normal position. The clock was moving pretty slow for me. It was 12:30 a.m., and I still had some time to pass.

I picked up my pen and pad, and tried to scribble the continuation to the story I was working on. I flipped to the page where I had left. I carefully read the last paragraph I had written, the pen dancing between my fingers. Even half an hour later, I hadn't put down a word. My mind, I discerned, wasn't fresh enough to give me something impressively creative.

I went out at last, to take a stroll across the strikingly big area outside the airport. Without an ounce of a doubt, I noticed that the place was powerfully magnetic. People from all walks of life could be seen around. It seemed like a global village, frantic and loud, with no care of whether it was day, or the dead of the night.

It was incredible that people exhibited different emotions at that one place. It was, for some, the happiest place because they were uniting with a loved one after many years, whereas for others, it was sad as their near ones were departing for another place. From the parking, to the pathways, to the washrooms and the eateries – they were all pristine.

Nevertheless, it wasn't the architecture that had astounded me as much as the difficulty to believe that Indians had been able to preserve its beauty. Because we have this reputation of being selfish and uncaring towards public property. We demolish almost everything that comes in our way.

It was charming for me to listen to the sound of the planes taking off and landing. Watching them so close was a mouthwatering experience. I remember going still and watching almost every plane that flew over my head. I wondered if ever in life I would get an opportunity to sit inside one and travel.

In my head, amidst dreams of a better tomorrow, I was pondering over the sort of life these ultra-rich get to live. For them, it must be like, they are born with an undisputed right to enjoy everything. And for us, it's like we can observe these rich people and feel envious, scheming up some extraordinary goals in our head and praying for things to work out. And in case they don't, we conveniently blame it on past life karma.

I moved towards the arrival gate, holding a placard in my hand. It was almost time for the lady to come, and I didn't want to be careless on the first ever chance. I could see a lot of people hustling around – security officers, ground workers, air hostesses (they were beautiful), pilots, and ground staff. Some looked spent and sleep deprived; others looked fresh and energetic. In the wee hours, as I stood before the exit with a cardboard having the name of this lady, there was suddenly a crowd that began to move out. These were the ones from the concerned flight, I guessed.

I raised the cardboard above my head for this lady to take notice. Especially whenever I saw a middle-aged lady or an older woman coming in my direction, I became more active, thinking she could be her. I would perhaps, at every chance, nervously point my finger at the name, nodding my head in a question. Most of them gestured a no with a smile. Rest ignored!

Then something enthralling happened, and you can sure call it a cliché. I saw an amazing young girl coming out from the exit gate. She was moving in my direction, and was so arresting that I had my mouth open. I was smitten by her charm. Her eyes were the most enticing I had ever witnessed in all my life. They were, to be very honest, brighter than the moon. Brighter than any star in the sky. I hadn't seen anything so perfect in my life before. Her impact was so overwhelming that I felt I had lost my voice for a moment.

The young lady was like all the missing parts of my heart walking on earth. I was breathing faster than ever before, and my heartbeat was beyond its normal rate. She was pushing the trolley with one hand and tucking her hair behind the ear with the other. She wore a pink top, dark blue jeans and a white pair of sneakers.

My hands, my eyes, the world around, everything had come to a stop. You can easily call her the most beautiful girl in the world. But only if… only if you choose to define beauty differently, unlike our generation does. That is, without rating a girl on her curves, on the size of her breasts, her hips, or how much she is exposing. You have to ignore all of it to see the eternal peace you feel on seeing her, that's what I am talking about.

She waved at me when she was about twenty steps away. I was so lost in her that I failed to respond. More so, because I could not believe that she was the one I had come to pick up and that I would be in her company for the next few hours.

In my absent-mindedness or by virtue of the girl leaving me all numb, the cardboard I was holding slipped out of my hands and hit the spectacles of the person standing next to me. His glasses fell down, cracking. He yelled in pain from the cut he got on his nose, and turned and gave a tight slap across my face. I landed straight onto the cold floor, wincing in pain from the slap.

When I got up, all I could see was this alluring girl arguing with the man. I stood up and went behind her, my hand on my cheek, as she ordered the burly man to apologize.

"But he broke my glasses. Doesn't this rascal know how to stand in a public place!" he shouted.

"No one would do that intentionally, of course. Better learn to keep your frustration in your pants and behave.... Apologize! Right now," she said with authority, looking at me in the end.

I didn't like the sympathetic tone in her voice at all. Her words hurt my machismo, in fact. Wasn't I supposed to be doing this, impressing her with how smart and strong I was!

Like a wounded tiger, I entered the scene again, trying to take charge of the situation.

"I will pay you for it, you uncivilized man! You don't know how to behave with a woman also. Tell me, how much is that local specs of yours for?" I said as he picked up the broken frame from the floor.

"Shut up, you beggar!" He walked away, looking at both of us in disgust.

How could someone be so rude, that too in front of her! With me, it was okay. I had a somewhat offending face. But how her, I wondered.

"Bloody moron!" she muttered.

I noticed how cute anger made her look. I was so mesmerized. She kept looking at the man angrily, as if she had lost a battle or missed a chance to nail him. Meanwhile, I kept looking at her pleasant face, with one hand still on my cheek that stung.

"Such things don't ever happen in Europe," she said. "People are valued there, and respected. India is still the same."

"Ma'am, say what you want to say about the guy. I am sure his rudeness has led you to be angry on him. But please don't spoil the country's name," I said.

"Oh yeah? And who do you think makes a country? It's people like us at the end of the day," she said and began picking up the placard that I had dropped.

And then it struck me. She had been walking in my direction, because she had read the placard. I gathered my wits to ask, "You are Upasna Sharma ji?"

She merely nodded, before asking me, "I suppose they have sent you to pick me up?"

"Yes ma'am. I have come to receive you. Sorry you had to be involved in this useless fight, ma'am," I said.

"Hmm. And please call me Upasna, not ma'am," she said. "I don't think I look that old."

"You are captivating," my tongue slipped.

"Excuse me?" Her beautiful eyes got bigger.

"This way, please," I said, grabbing the trolley. "The car is parked there."

"Who are you? An assistant to the driver?" she asked as we walked.

9

"No, I am your journey for the driver."

"What?"

"I mean, I am your driver for the journey."

"Are you even legally allowed to drive? You look so young. Not even 18!"

"I am, ma'am," I said, half laughing. "I have my license, and I passed the test for that. Didn't offer money like most people do."

"Hard to believe that."

"That I didn't bribe some officer?"

"No! Your age, and that you are working," she said. "Most importantly, I wonder how my parents trusted in your inexperience to get me. They are very particular about my safety otherwise."

I smiled. "Actually they didn't send me. My uncle, who drives your father's car, was supposed to come and pick you up. But he fell ill at the last moment, and maybe your parents were occupied, so he asked me to come instead."

"That's possible. My elder sister's wedding is scheduled to happen this Friday. They must be busy with the preparations."

"But you don't need to worry. I will drop you home safely. I promise," I said.

She bobbed her head, smiling.

I opened the door of the Toyota for her and went towards the car trunk to safely tuck in the luggage. Placing the trolley in its place, I quickly ran to the front and jumped into my seat.

Just as I put the key in its ignition slot, I heard her joyful voice, "Faaaantastic!"

I looked in the rear view mirror, surprised. She was holding a novel in her hand, flipping through the pages. It was a story I had written some two years ago and somehow had been able to convince a small publisher to publish it. Unfortunately, though, it was a huge flop. The last time I checked, it had sold only about 221 copies.

"This is one of my favourite stories. I'm so glad I found it here; I won't get bored now."

"Oh, some passenger must have forgotten it on the backseat," I lied, scared to confess the truth.

"Good for me," she said happily. "I have read this twice before and I really love the work."

"My feedback on this work is a little different. I didn't find the story too intriguing." This was my golden chance to get some first-hand feedback.

"Ahan!" She reacted, looking sharply at me. I am sure a driver saying he had read a novel was unexpected.

"Everyone is entitled to their opinion. For me, the way this writer Paarth mixes spirituality with all his substance, I love it. He enables the reader to vividly visualize the situation and that is commendable. He doesn't have a super good command over English maybe, but his content is original. He can use simple words and still be effective."

"The writer must have been glad to hear that, ma'am. That is such a constructive feedback," I said, pressing the gas, chuckling.

She smiled and said, "I wish I could meet him sometime. I would love to share this feedback with him in person."

Her words kindled me up. More than such a pretty girl wishing to meet me, I was happy to hear that someone really liked my work. There was at least one book lover on the planet who was finding happiness through my words. It was a big deal! Honestly speaking, I was always looking out for some sort of validation. This moment was like my wish being granted.

It was the first genuine feedback I had received from a reader and was something I wished to hear too. I was mostly looking at the book from my perspective before this. I never had the faintest idea of how my work is looked at by others. My friends or people around had not even bothered to read it, and even if they had, they would never tell me what they truly felt.

My parents could not read or write in English, so I could never ask them. To top it, the actual sales had been so bad, it could only have been destiny to have landed a reader in my taxi.

For a second, I was tempted to tell her that the writer of the book was driving her back home. But I chickened out almost instantly. What if she refused to believe me, and thought I was trying to be manipulative?

We crossed the Delhi border in the next forty-five minutes. She had asked me to switch the AC off and had half opened the window. Using the flash of her phone and the car light over her head on the back seat, she was busy reading the book. I was driving very attentively, but I wouldn't lie, noticing the empty road ahead of me, I did take every chance of looking at her.

She didn't raise her head to look at me even once, I noticed through the rear view mirror. And why on earth would she do that! She was a distant dream, yet I wished she could be my first reader forever.

I finally gathered some guts to ask politely, "I hope you don't mind my asking you something, ma'am."

"Only if you stop calling me ma'am. Call me Upasna," she said.

"I am sorry ma'am, but you are my customer. I think, the more respect I give to people like you, the more likely I am to attract a steady clientele."

"That's a good thought. I appreciate it," she said, smiling pleasantly. "But this word 'ma'am' makes me feel like I am some really old lady. I am 22, for god's sake, and I want people to treat me like that too."

"Oh yes!" I muttered. That was going to be my question. Her age. Thankfully, she had herself told me. I smiled in joy, softly whistling.

"So? What was your question?" she asked

"Umm... my question," I stuttered. I was trying to think of something now, and quickly.

"Where did you first find this book, Upasna ji?" I quickly covered up.

"Upasna... not Upasna ji," she said. "That's even worse than ma'am. And I found this book in a bookstore in Bangalore."

I was pleasantly surprised to hear that. This meant my publisher had taken the pain of distributing the book to various locations. This was my chance to dig deeper.

"Was it a big book store or a smaller one? And what about the location? Posh or average?" I fired questions, wondering about my publisher's brand equity.

"Big... small... posh... poor... What are you investigating?" She seemed a little taken aback. "I hope you aren't another victim of Savdhan India, and this is not some copy used in a murder."

I realized what a silly question I had just asked. I hadn't told her I was a writer keen to learn about my books' visibility.

I laughed and then covered up, saying, "Just for time pass."

She was left rather puzzled. I chose to stay quiet for some time, sure I'd end up making her uncomfortable if I shot some more silly questions. It had barely been a couple of minutes when I looked into the rear view mirror, and saw her eyes closed, the book on her chest. It looked as if a beautiful ocean had gone to rest. I focused on driving, trying to cover as much distance as possible. The next I heard her voice was when day had broken, and she got up all hungry, asking to stop for breakfast. It was around 06:30 a.m. when we paused at a dhaba near Karnal. Just as she was about to go ahead, she politely offered me a hundred rupee note. I shook my head, refusing to accept it.

"Come on! Your breakfast has to be on me," she retorted.

"Upasna Ji…" I said.

She glowered at me, widening her eyes, pointing at my mistake.

I tried really hard, her name just didn't come out of my mouth without the 'ji'.

"Sorry," I managed to whisper, to which she smiled.

I tried to say out her name again, but when it didn't happen, I just went with being vague. "It hurts my self-esteem to accept anything beyond the price for my services. I whole heartedly thank you for being so generous, but no, thank you. Moreover, I am carrying my food along."

"Oh really? Show me what you have," she said with a broad smile, happily ignoring every other thing I had just said.

"But…"

"Show me... show me," she was adamant.

I leapt forward and opened the dashboard, grabbing my round steel tiffin. There were two paranthas wrapped up in a Punjabi newspaper.

"Unwrap it. Quick!" she said.

I was feeling rather embarrassed as the rich girl, I thought, would consider this form of food presentation so non-classy and stupid.

On the contrary, she snatched the tiffin from my hands. Quickly, she took a bite and was in awe of the thing.

"Who made this? Your mom?" she said as she chewed it slowly, savouring it.

"No," I said, smiling. "My mother makes much better paranthas than I do."

"Don't tell me you made this." She stopped chewing in shock. "Your wife would be so lucky, huh."

'Then why let such an ideal proposition like me slip out of your hands?' I said in my head, looking at her eating. 'You like my book, the food I prepared, what else does a girl want in her man?' my mind went on imagining.

My eyes were fixed on her, and I had lost control over my smile again. In no time, I noticed that she was done with the parantha.

She was actually licking her fingertips while she said, "Had homemade Indian food after two years. What a welcome! All thanks to you, I must say!" she said, very delighted, handing the tiffin back.

"You have a big heart. It is a pleasure to be of help," I replied.

She convinced me to have tea with her, for treating her to such a delightful breakfast. I stood leaning against the door of my car, having the tea, while she was walking around sipping it. Out of nowhere, she brought me a packet of chips and a diary milk chocolate.

You haven't come from Germany. You must be from heaven, I suppose.

Just as we were about to enter Ambala, an over-speeding white SUV from the other side of the road came jumping over the divider and rammed into a lorry just ahead of us. The lorry had overtaken us a few seconds back. The collision led to a huge smashing sound, dragging the involved vehicles to almost the edge of the road. A motorcyclist too had been hit, and flew up like a toy. All of this happened within the blink of an eye.

I pressed the brakes and my car skidded towards the right for a few metres. Upasna was almost shivering on the backseat, crying. She was breathing heavily, and had her hand on her heart. I could hear mine pounding. Almost all the vehicles around us were screeching to a halt. I kept my head on the steering, catching my breath. It had been a terrible, terrible accident, and if not for the lorry having overtaken us, it could have been us. Everything before my eyes was spinning at the very thought of what could have happened.

After my heartbeat came to normal, I looked out and saw a pool of blood. I almost jumped out hearing the screams of the victims. Most people ran out from their vehicles and gathered around the site. There were small pieces of glass spread everywhere on the road. No one dared to help as a lifeless, bloodied arm dangled out from a window. Someone surely had died.

People immediately called for an ambulance. I leapt forward and pulled the door open, putting the hand back inside the car first. It scared the hell out of me in doing that. Then, I dragged the body from the back seat of the SUV out. My hands and my shirt were soaked in blood in no time. The person had lost so much blood that I could not imagine what would happen. I was hoping for someone to help me, but everyone just kept looking on as a spectator. Someone finally came forward, helping the driver out of the lorry. He had a gaping wound on his forehead and was bleeding profusely. A few people stood in the distance, I assumed around the motorcyclist. I heard someone pronounce him dead out loud. I meanwhile managed to pull out other people from the car. They were in complete panic and understood nothing. The one who had died was a middle-aged lady. There was an elderly couple who were literally in blood, and in shock.

The man on the driving seat was also bleeding very badly and I, with help from another person, brought him to the corner of the road. In this short timespan, an ambulance arrived and quickly took the victims away. The police reached the site in no time and enquired about the accident from the witnesses present there.

With my hands, clothes and almost everything soaked in blood, I jogged towards my own car. In the whole hustle-bustle, I had completely forgotten about Upasna. She had been seeing all this from inside the car, scared and traumatized. I opened the car door and looked around for my bottle of water. It was empty. I opened the car trunk to check if I had a spare one. There wasn't a drop of water in any bottle. Upasna understood what I was looking for and came out with some water. I gestured towards the wide road divider and led the way. I put my hands forward and she poured out water for me to wash my hands.

Then I took out the bag I usually kept in the car trunk for emergencies, and changed my clothes behind a tree. I left the clothes soaked in blood there itself. I was scared at the thought of wearing them back again. I just didn't want them anymore. I took the deepest breath, occupying my seat back again. I looked at my hands and I couldn't believe what I had done. The flashes of the entire episode ran through my mind. I seemed to have lost all my energy. Upasna's shivering hand came to rest on my shoulder, assuring. I looked back to see her eyes full of understanding and sympathy.

I gave her a smile, but I was sure she saw through it. Saw how disturbed I was. I pressed on the accelerator, heading towards the destination, looking out for some water on the way. I stopped at a dhaba and sat down on a chair, my eyes closed. I was rattled, flummoxed and still in disbelief of what I had seen. Human life can seem so cheap sometimes. Had the lorry not overtaken our car, we could have been the victims. It was a fortunate narrow escape.

Upasna came and sat opposite me. "That was intense," she said, breaking the ice. "I hope you are fine now."

Even after drinking four glasses of water, I realized my mouth was still dry. Picking the jug and pouring more water in my glass, I replied with a nod.

"Do you want me to order something for you?" she asked.

"I don't think I'll be able to swallow anything," I said.

"Take your time. Don't rush. Drive forth only when you are comfortable," she said, soothingly.

"Umm...." I was feeling nauseous after seeing so much flesh and blood.

"You are a brave man. Thanks for helping those people." she said.

It was nice of her to appreciate me, but I had no answers. I wasn't in the right frame of mind.

"Let's go!" I said after some time, thinking this would never get better if I kept sitting like this.

AT 11:00 A.M., WE REACHED CHANDIGARH.

After a long silence of about an hour, she finally spoke, "How could you gather the guts to pull out those people when the rest of the crowd was so ignorant and numb?"

"Even I don't know. I am so scared of blood, to be honest. I have even fainted on seeing blood in the past. But when I realized someone could die if we delayed, it almost made me forget everything and help them," I said.

"Wow! I think that's how circumstances bring out the best in us," she said. Then she cleared her throat and said in a more serious tone, "Please don't show any nervousness in front of my parents, or they will feel intimidated or whatever."

"Sure! You live in Sector 9A? That is what my uncle told me. Can you please guide me to the exact location of your place?"

"Sure," she replied, and in ten minutes, thanks to her navigation skills, we were outside a dwelling that looked like a poster house from fancy magazines. The look was entirely metallic and there were huge glass windows that added to its sophistication. On the ramp were cemented light brown tiles that shone like mirrors. The front door opened with a biometric scanner. Once parked right in front of the house in the driveway, I started unloading her luggage. Her relatives and two German shepherds excitedly jumped out to welcome her.

"Chhotu, keep these bags inside the hall," said one elderly lady, who seemed to be the mother.

I folded my hands, saying yes, and started with the task. I tried picking as many bags as I could in one go. From a driver, I had dawned the role of a coolie now. As I stepped inside, a delightful fragrance greeted me. I turned to look at a small lush green garden with flower beds on the right. It was then that I realized that both the dogs were following me. Maybe they were aware of the protocol I was supposed to follow. One of them was smelling all the bags one by one from behind, the other my feet and knees as I marched. I cut down on my speed in fear. Their steady frames made them seem like mini beasts who could tear me apart into pieces within seconds.

A brown plaid sofa adorned the huge drawing room. It looked expensive, and very classy. One wall was completely devoted to family pictures. A sleek and vibrant chandelier hung from the middle of the ceiling. It exuded taste and warmth in all its crystal chains. I hadn't ever seen such an astonishing place to live in. In fact, I had never even assumed that someone would have these things in their homes. These things looked more for grand hotels.

"Do they have a factory of notes or what?" I mumbled, staring around, bewildered.

I was shifting the luggage to the specified place, but somewhere in my heart, I was waiting for her to come back and say a word. I know it was too much to ask for. But all I could hear was her voice, speaking delightfully and laughing from some room. She didn't come. She had vanished from the sight, and I left the place after collecting my due.

The moment I was all by myself in the car, my mind began drifting to the accident again. I wondered how strange life really is! It gives us reasons to be happy, throwing surprises, and not always the pleasant ones. I consoled myself for whatever I had got, and forgot all about bidding her goodbye. I didn't know if I would ever see her again, but I did know that her picture would be painted in my eyes forever.

I reached home and slept, having been up the whole night, and having lived through a near-death experience. My house was as small, plain and boring as one could think of. I was feeling a strange sense of loss. I was well aware it was a typical teenage feeling that takes over and stays for a little while.

I felt sorry for myself, for I was never going to see her again. She was beautiful, kind, benevolent and considerate. Needless to say, my best customer forever.

I spent the following three days driving a newlywed couple from Chandigarh to Manali and back. They were quite unlike any shy Indian pair, as one would expect. The man especially seemed to be some kind of a predator. The way he could not resist himself from kissing his wife, and the sound effects they together produced, raised weird questions in my head. I wondered how they were surviving without sex before marriage in the first place.

The man would shamelessly press the breasts of his wife anytime he felt like. He didn't care about the cars moving around and people putting their heads out of the windows to check them out. The girl would only stop him when the breasts were on the verge of popping out, adjusting her T-shirt quickly. I requested them so many times to not indulge in such things, or the police would question me for their activities. But every time I issued a polite request, I was greeted with his middle finger.

Since their trip didn't have more than a twelve-hour stay at a hotel, and it was mainly a road trip, the couple's frustration seemed to be rising with the passage of time. The guy requested me many times to park the car at some isolated place, and leave for 20-25 minutes. They were ready to pay extra for that, they said. I bluntly declined every single time. Because rules are rules, and my car seats were not going to witness the adventure they were looking for. I had no intentions of cleaning up their mess after the whole escapade.

This guy finally gave a tight slap across my face when I refused to listen to his request on the last highway to Chandigarh. I swear, I thought, being a failed author was better than driving sex freaks around the city, who could hit you anytime.

I was so angry, I stopped the car on the side and called him out of the car. Before I could warn him or as much as say a word, that man started beating the hell out of me, leaving me with no time to react. I was barely a match, and the next thing I know, he had tossed me into the bushes. I lay there for close to two hours before regaining consciousness. I woke up in pain, a deep bruise under my left eye and the eye so swollen up that I couldn't see anything with it. I had bled from the nose, I guess, because there was some dried blood on the upper lip. I hurried onto the road to check my car. Thankfully, it was there, but the key was missing.

With tears in my eyes and a severe pain on my face, I began looking for the keys everywhere – inside the car, on the road and the place I had gotten up from. The incident had scared the demons out of me. My entire body was shivering in dismay, as the couple had fled. Even a meager sum of five hundred rupees meant the world to me, and here I had lost almost seven to eight thousand rupees to this couple. How would we run our home this month, I thought.

Not able to find a way out of this situation, I called my best friend Kartik. He picked up on the first ring itself, and could sense the heaviness in my voice. He had a long list of questions for me, naturally, but I shouted at him to bury all his questions and get me a key maker on the Chandigarh–Manali road at the earliest.

Kartik arrived in about an hour-and-a-half, as fast as his Honda Activa could bring him and the key maker. I had pushed the car to the side of the road in the meantime, and was sitting on the bonnet, waiting for him. I explained the whole situation to him while he gave me some first aid and the key maker did his work. I was crying inconsolably, because I knew everything about the scene waiting at home.

My parents and I had fought over the smallest issues in the world. In everything wrong I reported, they would hold me guilty. Because we were financially so restrained, if my judgment led to a loss of fortune, which in this case had happened, my body would be their punching bag, to get rid of the anger.

Kartik suggested me to file a police complaint against the couple. I told him I knew nothing about them as they had approached me at the taxi stand near the railway station, my usual place of waiting for customers. After paying off the key maker, he asked me to reach at the chowk where he had his grocery shop. It took us a while to be there, but when we did, he came to my car, having stolen ten thousand rupees from the shop's money box.

I couldn't believe my eyes for the first few seconds. My best friend, who I looked up to as an inspiration, as an angel, was actually stealing without guilt! Anyhow, my heart melted at the thought that he had done all of it to save me from trouble.

"I can't take this money, brother," I said as he tossed the money in my lap. "This will save me, but what about you. I cannot buy my happiness at the cost of pushing you into trouble."

"Listen, Paarth! I know what I am doing. My father is out of town for fifteen days. I'll figure out ten thousand different ways to cover this."

"In case that doesn't happen, he will throw you out of the house. You do know that na?" I said.

"You don't have to think about that. I am not stealing his money for the first time, you see," he said ever so casually.

"You have been doing this before as well?" I asked, shocked. This wasn't the Kartik I thought I knew inside out.

"Past three years," he confessed with pride. "And what do you think? From where do I arrange money for the movies that I take you out for every weekend?"

"What the—"

"And also, the book you published, from where did I arrange the money for it? I am sure you don't think RBI approved my loan."

I heaved a deep breath, and released it only after a few seconds. "Now I know why it didn't work. I was using someone's hard-earned money in the wrong way for a pious task."

"Listen, you moral science test case, when life doesn't behave right with right people, take the course you get. That's all I have learnt," Kartik said.

"Boss, the day you get caught, I am sure I'll be dragged along. They will presume I have been encouraging you to do this."

"Big deal! Isn't that what friendship is? Getting your ass kicked together?"

"Ahan! All prisoners should be brothers by that logic."

"Where are you headed now? Home?" Kartik quickly changed the subject.

I shook my head and realized I still had pain here and there. "I'll wait till evening at the taxi stand itself. If I get any local passengers, I will take them around. That will mainly give some time to my swollen eye to look better."

"Better have something to eat too. I see you losing weight," he said, scanning me. "You haven't been taking care of your diet, I suppose."

I nodded, half hugged him and went my way.

☙3

I REACHED HOME THAT EVENING, PARKING MY CAR IN THE EMPTY plot in our locality. To my surprise, there was an Audi standing right in front of the gate. I looked around, wondering why dunces cannot use common sense while parking their vehicles. I entered irked, and my mother came running towards me. The urgency told me maybe she had a hint about the incident.

"What happened?" I asked, just to make sure.

Adjusting her dupatta on her shoulders, she said, "There is a Madam ji waiting for you since afternoon."

Her eyes stopped on me just then, and she caught me by the chin. "How did this happen to you?"

"Nothing! Had a brawl with someone driving rash. He was drunk," I lied.

"Why can't you ignore people and mind your own business?" she said.

"Which Madam ji has come?" I asked, to evade any further grilling.

"Malhotra ji's daughter."

"Which Malhotra ji?" I asked, displeased as if I was supposed to know all Malhotra jis in the world.

"Idiot, the same for whom your uncle works. The one you went to pick up from Delhi."

"Upasna ji? What's she doing here?" I said, walking quickly towards the sitting area.

I folded my hands before Upasna as she looked at me with a smile. She immediately kept her phone down and stood folding her hands. There was sweat on her face, I could notice. I was sure she wasn't very used to sitting under just a fan on such hot days. I couldn't help but wonder how modestly she had waited in our tiny drawing room in this heat, without an air conditioner, or even a cooler, just for me.

"Please sit… please," I requested, feeling guilty at having made her wait for so long.

"What happened to your face?" she asked, concerned.

"Nothing. That's regular for us."

"What do you mean by regular? This is serious. Look at your face."

"It's ok now. I saw a doctor and have taken first aid," I half lied.

She murmured something looking at me, without blinking. I couldn't understand a word of it though.

"I am so sorry you had to sit here without an AC," I said.

"That is completely fine," she said. "You don't have to say sorry for this. And please have a seat. Don't remain standing."

I quickly pulled a plastic chair and sat before her, feeling nervous. My mother came and stood against the door frame of the drawing room. She did not come to listen to what was going on, but to make sure she was there, ready to sprint and get anything that Upasna ji might need.

"You know why I am here, right?" she asked me.

I didn't answer. I smirked, understanding everything.

After a minute of smiling back, she finally said, "So you can keep your book in my bag, writing a personalized message for me, but cannot admit in person that you are the one I have been looking for?"

While we had stopped at the dhaba on our return journey from Delhi, I had written a small message for Upasna on the book while she was away for a few minutes and kept it in her bag. Naturally, I was expecting her to know that I was the author of the work she had praised. The message read:

Dear Reader,

I am extremely happy to learn that you found this book worth your time. Yours is the first feedback I have received on my work, and I cannot put in words how special it's going to remain to me. Whatever you have said is going to be taken very seriously. I'll ensure my best to keep my work as original and spiritual as possible.

Not to forget, I am putting in my sincerest efforts to come up with better works. Hoping my simple English soon turns extraordinary.

Your Driver

I replied, "I didn't have the confidence actually... to... you know... tell..."

"Strange! You can pull off a fantastic book at this young age, yet lack the confidence to say that it belongs to you."

"I am actually not... used to taking credit, or coming forward much. Probably that is why I am a writer."

"I am sure you can be a good actor as well. Anyone else would surely have gotten carried away with the praise and that would have clearly shown on their face, but not you."

"That's supposed to be sarcasm, right?" I was confused.

"I mean it, Mr Paarth Avasthi." She grinned and I could barely nod. What else was I supposed to do in such a situation!

"I'll take your leave now. It's getting late for me," she said, getting up. "I have already bothered aunty a lot while waiting for you." My mother shook her head politely. "But I really didn't want to leave without meeting you." Her smile was beatific as she finished talking.

How can this conversation end so soon? My heart screamed. It had just started and I wanted more. I wanted to shout that out.

"You came all the way for this?" I still couldn't believe my luck. "For telling me what you just did?"

She smiled again, nodding her head. Then she stopped suddenly, a spark in her eyes. "Can we have a picture together, please?"

"That will be an honour for me," I simply said, not knowing how else I could react.

She came and stood next to me, raising her phone for a selfie. I looked at her eyes in the camera, living every breath of the thought that she stood so close to me. A strand of her hair fell on my shoulder. Her fragrance was startling.

My mother's expressions were quite picturesque too, I noticed. I would certainly have clicked her photo or invited her to get clicked with us, had I not been so lost myself. I am sure she was thinking – a girl who my brother-in-law works for, storms into my house, waits for three hours to take a picture with my good for nothing son. Why?

She looked at the picture she had taken admiringly, and

turned to say, "Keep writing! This was a fantastic book. I'll look forward to more from you."

Just before slipping out of the gate, she cautiously handed over a chit of paper to me. I buried it inside my pocket, saving it from my mother's eyes. She waved at me and left in her car. I turned back and closed the gate of the house behind me. Now it was my mother's turn. She stood there red-faced, waiting for me.

"Can I ask what is all this? What is this new thing?"

"Come on, Maa! She just read the book written by your son, liked it, and came to get a photo clicked with me. Even she knows this boy is going to go a long way. You should be a proud mother today." I tried to tell her what it really was.

"How much has your piece of shit earned us, can you tell me?" was all that she said.

"Maa, I am just starting out. It will take time for me to reach some place you can be proud of. People will slowly read my work. Word of mouth will generate, sales will rise, and then the book will start giving me some income to boast of."

"You know; it is these kind of girls that make you act crazy. No shame, nothing! Just because they are rich, they think they can enter anybody's house!"

My heart was now giving up convincing her. "Rather, 'these kind of girls' understand what it is to be a writer. They respect someone's efforts, unlike some others who don't even try to understand."

"Ahan! How much money did she give you then?"

"Why would she give me any money?"

"Exactly! Better don't endorse and encourage anything that cannot better our financial condition."

"Maa, money is not everything."

"Till you don't have enough to live comfortably, it certainly is," she said with finality. "And listen, boy, if this turns out anything more than what you have just said, and it gives us trouble in any way in the future, consider yourself dead."

She went inside her room after issuing the warning. I was more than happy to be alone, and took the chit out of my pocket. She had left her number on it with a small line:

Text me whenever you find time. I'll be waiting.

My happiness knew no bounds. A girl had given me her number, without my asking for it, and even asked me to text her. Oh my god! *Makes me sound like another desperate fellow, doesn't it?* Music played in my head. Mixing steps of bhangra with Nagin dance, I jumped around the room in joy. Immediately, I called Kartik and told him all that had just happened. He warned me to put the phone down and not bother him, because he thought I was fooling around. There was no way he was ready to believe that Upasna herself had come and reached out to talk over phone. But when I swore over writing, he was left heartbroken.

"This world is so unjust," were his last words before he hung up.

I was still thinking what happened to him, when he rang me back.

"Now what?" I asked.

"Whatever, and I literally mean whatever you both talk about, I must be aware about it," he said, like an order.

"Dude, it's my personal life," I said, anticipating what was coming.

"Personal life! Personal life? The friend for whom I made the biggest sacrifices in life tells me today that it's his personal life!" he said dramatically.

"Stop being a cartoon, Kartik. You know me enough. I don't play around with girls, so there won't be any spice for you."

"Can you get any of her sisters to talk to me?" he asked after a pause.

"I don't work for thieves," I said, just as dramatically.

FINISHING WITH MY DINNER AND CLEARING OFF THE KITCHEN AFTER that, I locked the main gate and ensured I had completed everything and won't be disturbed by anyone now. Then I wrote the first text to her.

Hi! This is Paarth. You can save this number.

Hi!:) Been waiting for your message. Thank you! How have you been?

I am good, Upasna ji. How are you doing?

Again this Ji :(Didn't I tell you my age?

I am sorry. This will take some time.

You have a very cute smile, by the way. Don't take it otherwise.

Surely not! Thank you. You have great eyes.

When is the next book coming?

I thought for a while about it. I didn't want to sound negative. I didn't want to lie either. I wrote back, giving the most honest answer

Next year maybe, if a traditional publisher accepts my proposal. Or when I have enough money to market.

Oh! I won't mind reading the unpublished manuscript. You can always share.

Thanks!:) I did need someone who could give me honest feedback.

I am happy I can be of help.

You are kind. :)

You are inspiring. Working at a very young age. Simultaneously following your passion as well. You are someone to stand by.

I took a screenshot of her message and saved it to favourites in my phone gallery, and then I replied.

I'll remember these words whenever I feel demotivated. I am sure they will get me back on track.

:) You are too modest. Not many can be that way.

I haven't achieved much to be arrogant.

You will be something soon; I can bet my money on that.

That's tooooooo much faith.

In someone who will prove his worth.

What if he doesn't?

Then I'll believe that his time is yet to come.

True that!

Good night! I'll ping you tomorrow, Paarth. Up to something.

Peaceful sleep, Upasna. Good night!

:) :) :)

My instinct said she was impressed by me. I read our texts like a thousand times that night. My heart kept poking me to write 'I Love You' to her. But that would have been too much, and too early. So every time my heart convinced me to write it, my mind told me she would get scared and run off. So while I was playing this game of typing 'I Love You' and erasing it, Kartik messaged me.

Now that you are a big writer, favourite of many young girls, why would people like us be given importance anymore?

*Especially when you hang
up? Absolutely! Fuck off.*

Suck my c*ck

God of small things!

When reality hits people, they generally run out of answers. I did not receive any message from Kartik thereafter. I had been quite taken aback with his reaction on call, and now, he seemed to have gone deep into the state of self-realization, or so I hoped.

I dozed off sometime later, reading my conversation with Upasna. Those simple ordinary texts gave me extraordinary joy. When I woke up the next morning, I found the phone on the floor. It must have slipped off my hands when I dozed off. I picked it up to find its screen broken. It was working, I checked, and that was enough for me.

While driving to work, I kept checking for her text to arrive. Every time my phone beeped, I thought it was her. Needless to say, I was acting like a teenager. Like talking to her was the only thing that mattered now. I was convinced that I was in love with her and that I wanted her. All of a sudden, Upasna was an obsession that had taken over me completely.

Until noon, neither did I get any passenger, nor her message. A plethora of questions ran in my head. I prayed she had not lost interest in me or found any message of mine offensive. But all those thoughts aside, I did not lose hope. The number of times I looked at the phone screen didn't go down. In the end, my patience finally bore fruit. Her message came beeping, bringing a smile on my face.

Guten Morgen, Herr Schriftstellar!:)

What does that even mean, I wondered!

I quickly typed back,

Translate please! :/

That means, Good Morning.
Mr Writer!:)

I think the sun is not in the east anymore.
It's right above our heads, expecting us to
be in the middle of our tasks.

Hahaha. My father talks like that. I
just woke up, by the way. This is my
usual time on holidays.

Okay :) Good morning!

How has the day been so far?

*Have been in my car, writing my book
and looking out for passengers.*

Any luck so far?

*Seems like a bad day today. Both
with writing and driving.*

Oh no! Can I help in any way?

Just tell me that you love me and can't live without me was
what I wanted to type and send off to her. But I knew I was
going ahead of myself there. So I had to be careful.

Thank you so much for the concern. :)

I chose to sound as decent as possible.

*Would I have to take an appointment
if I want to meet you?*

"What? Seriously! Did I just read that right? She wants
to meet me? *Me*?" I said to myself, re-reading the message.

*Please don't embarrass me by saying that!
It would be an honor to see you in person.*

I again chose to sound formal and decent.

Okay then! We meet today! Done?

Surely done! But when and where?

Not at your home, for sure! :p

Haha! Wherever you feel comfortable, I am on. Just let me know.:)

Sukhna Lake. At 6?

Done.

I kissed my phone with some passion, and screamed that it was the best day of my life. What more could I wish for! I folded my hands and looked up with a smile, thanking god. The first girl who I had felt for so intensely had come forward and asked to see me. Unbelievable! From head to toe, every inch of my skin was feeling exhilarated.

I REACHED THE LAKE NESTLED IN THE FOOTHILLS OF THE SHIVALIK range quite ahead of her. The golden hue of the dusk shimmered through the placid waters and a stream of joggers hurried along to savour the fresh air. Visitors clicked photos with a steel structure with the insignia of the city – open hand, and of course, the renowned heritage tree.

The picturesque waterfront adorned with the melodious chirruping of birds and a serene atmosphere made me forget everything else. This place felt so full of life, with families thronging the promenade, the Lakeview Cafeteria, and shops at jetty for a boat ride. People ambled on grass, children frolicked around, while many meditated in tranquility.

I reached the Garden of Silence there, a space cut out for meditation at the far end of it. It is a designed garden with stepped layers around the statue of seated Buddha. The place was absolutely silent and deserted. Upasna also reached there fifteen minutes later.

She was in her black yoga pants and a white Adidas T-shirt, her hair tied in a pony. That sporty look was yet another captivating side of hers. The way she walked towards me, flashing a wide smile, appearing full of life, I am sure even the best of my words could not have perfectly captured it. It felt as if all my desires had taken a human form and decided to surprise me. I had lost control over my eyes again. They were glued to her face, it seemed. She had such a tranquilizing effect on me that my body went numb once again. I could see nothing, but her. I could feel nothing, but her. I could hear nothing, but her.

"I am sorry for being just a little late. And when I say 'just a little late', you must consider yourself very lucky." She laughed as she sat down.

"So you wake up late, you turn up late... everything late," I said, looking deep into her bright eyes.

"Except for having food," she said, laughing again, extending her hand for a high five.

I smiled and looked at my feet, thinking about something. "Don't you feel awkward sitting here with a driver?" I said. I dared not look at her, but really wanted to voice my thoughts. "A rich handsome fellow should be your first choice; don't you think?"

"I am trying my luck on a very talented young man, who might turn out to be the next big thing."

I grinned at her confidence. Her statement saved my self-esteem from falling.

"And by the way, this talented fellow is no less handsome, get that!" she added, pointing her finger at me.

"You are definitely over-rating me." I laughed. Even my mother had never said that I was handsome.

"My instincts can't bluff me. They never have, and they never will," she said just as sharply and confidently.

I was mesmerized by the go-getter kind of girl she seemed to be.

"My responsibility was to warn you, young lady. I am not going to take any blame later."

"Your future prospects haven't intrigued me. Tomorrow is a mystery, I know. It's your innocence that encourages me to talk to you. You don't find such purity in the world anymore. It's rare, you know. Quite scarce."

I beamed at her, wondering how easily she could express what she felt, without being worried about how the other person might turn out to be. A majority of people, no matter how sure they are of the other person's worth, don't acknowledge it most of the time. But Upasna... she was unique. She was the complete opposite of how the world behaved. She had no fear in her mind. She lived with zero insecurities. She had no ego that could serve as an obstacle. She was a gem.

"Okay! Now start with telling me everything important about you," she said.

Things were going way too quick, I realized. The style in which our confabulation started felt as if we were on a mutually agreed upon date kind of a thing. I only hoped there was no conspiracy against me and decided to go with the flow.

"Umm. Everything in my life is quite insignificant. But yeah, I am a school dropout. Maa is a homemaker. My father worked as a driver before suffering a paralysis attack, which left half of his body non-functional. We live in a small house which you have already seen. And after my father suffered the stroke, I am the sole earning member in the family."

"No siblings?" she asked.

"Had an elder sister. But she succumbed to dengue when she was ten."

"Oh, I am really sorry to hear that," she said. "I am sure she is in a better place."

"Peaceful and safe, wherever she must be," I said, rubbing my hands.

A brief silence ensued for a while, both of us not knowing how to react.

"So what interesting bits do you have to share? I am sure your story is more interesting and less stupid than mine," I said trying to change the sullen atmosphere.

"Boss, the sort of life you have lived, Bollywood would make a film on it one day. Just keep doing what you're doing and you'll see what happens."

"I have never been praised so much ever before." I laughed.

"Of course, because our society is miserable. It takes joy in others' pain," she said.

"Okay, okay! No more bashing. Let's get to your introduction now," I said, quite eager to know her better.

"Well, I finished my schooling here itself in India. Always have been a class topper. From nursery to twelfth. Always. Past two years, I have been in Germany doing my engineering. We have a family business of metals, and both my parents, my uncle and aunt look after it."

"That's huge!" I said. "Plan on getting a German citizenship?"

"Or American maybe," she quickly answered, like she had given it some thought already. "Haven't taken a call yet."

Such insanely huge dreams and the confidence with them spoke out loud, that they were dreamt to be accomplished.

Perks of money maybe. But then, that's also where my mind stopped working. If she had plans to settle abroad, then she would get married abroad. What am I doing here then? Helping her to spend her holidays?

"I am sure you have a girlfriend! Am I right?"

"No," I said, "you are not." There was a sudden change in my tone. "I haven't spoken to anyone as much as I have done with you."

"Come on, that has to be the biggest lie in the world."

My mind had now started contemplating with the idea that maybe she was just playing around with me, passing her time. "Don't you understand I said no!" I almost shouted on her comments. The immaturity in me had awakened.

"What's wrong with you?" she asked. "We can leave if you aren't feeling good?" she further added on seeing my expression unchanged.

How stupid of me to have behaved in such an insane manner. I felt like hitting my head on a wall. Why am I feeling so possessive and acting stupid? She will run away and I'll keep regretting later. Patience is the key, I reminded myself.

"You got scared, right?" I said, my eyebrows raised. I was smartly trying to give an impression that I had been acting, and with the change in her expression, I was convinced I had convinced her.

"The way you spoke, anyone would get scared," she said nervously.

"Sensitive topic, you know. Single guy. No girl to look after him. Life like an Indian farmer. No field. No rain." I fractured my English to make her laugh, and succeeded in my motive.

"Indian farmer! No field. No rain…" She clapped her hands, laughing uncontrollably.

"You should, in the first place, think it out rationally, Upasna. Come on! I mean, I am an *Bhartiya londa* with whom this can be a very realistic possibility."

"Achha! Explain the rationale behind this," she said, still laughing.

"Okay, so the first obstacle is the sex ratio, of course. And then these extra intelligent boys who date multiple girls at a given time, leaving no one single around us. Every second guy is without a girl, but all girls are in a relationship. Can you explain where the girls are going? To monkeys?"

She laughed even more. "What a brilliant justification for your failure!"

"Hey, look! I wasn't ever…"

Upasna's mobile interrupted me. She pulled it out from her pocket, and my eyes fell over the caller's name. It flashed 'Dad', along with two hearts and a family picture. The call lasted for a few seconds, with her saying nothing more than hmm and okay every now and then. As she hung the phone, I asked out of curiosity, "That was your family photo, right?"

"Oh yes," she said, scrolling to the gallery and taking the photo out. Pointing at every member, she told me who was who. Also, she did not miss out on explaining how much she was loved by everyone, and her one favourite memory with every member in the photo.

That's how all girls are supposed to be. So attached to their family that they need just an opportunity or a trigger to talk of them. Guys on the other hand are quite the opposite. They, most of the time, don't want to talk about family and related stuff. Not that they don't love their blood relations; just that they find it boring to discuss it.

I listened to Upasna quite enthusiastically. What can a poor helpless guy do! Cut a girl when she is talking of her family and you shall know.

"Show me your family picture," she then said.

"I... I don't have any," I said, honestly.

"This is not as difficult as finding a girlfriend, you know," she said.

"Yeah," I replied in a very dull voice, stealing my eyes from her.

"Oh hero, family photo?" she asked, tapping my shoulder.

I did not know what to say. What could I tell her of my relationship with my family? "I seriously don't have a family photo," I finally replied.

"Why? What happened?" she asked.

"I don't have a way with my parents. We don't get along very well." It wasn't that hard to confess.

"Why is that, if you don't mind sharing?" she asked concerned.

"I don't know. It has always been like this," I said. "It's natural, I guess. Right from the day that I can remember, I haven't seen us being very good to each other."

"You don't love your parents?"

"Hey, I certainly do! It's the expression that is missing from my side. From their side, I can't say the same. Maybe they really don't want me."

"Don't you think that's too much negativity inside you, without even trying to find the truth?"

"I would call that burning desperation. My heart craves for a hug from my father," I explained. "He has never taken me in his arms. Never ever! Whenever I see my friends' fathers hugging them, cheering them and standing by them, I feel bad for myself. Wondering what wrong have I done to be so undeserving."

"Did you try and hug him ever?" she asked, very innocently.

I looked up at her, thinking deep in my heart how I had never even tried this.

"Nope," I said, very clearly.

"May be he is waiting for you to make a move," she said. "May be he craves for your love and affection in the same way when he sees his friends being hugged by their sons."

I was blank at that moment. "How do I even do that? He has never expressed his love to me. Never even tried, I mean."

"If he has never expressed love to you, why didn't you try? Why did you also become something you did not like?" she said. "Maybe the situations that he faced in life made him so tough on the outside, you know."

"It isn't what you are thinking, Upasna. It's not like I haven't tried. I… uhh… have tried doing it. Umm…" I didn't know how to justify it to her.

"Don't you think each time you went to him, you went with a condition in your heart? If he was going to reciprocate the warmth you had decided to show, this goes on, or else it would be back to its original cold form?" Her question hit my heart hard.

I thought for a while and decided she wouldn't be able to understand me, like several others around me. She too, like all my relatives, would blame me for everything. No point explaining, I decided.

"Tell me," she insisted. "Why do you have to have conditions with your parents? That too with love?"

"Don't you think being an elder, it was his responsibility to take care of the growing distance between us? Wasn't it on him to see to the fact that I needed him more than he needed me? Because I am his child… his very own blood," I said, like a rebel. Her questions had managed to irk me, because she had touched a raw nerve.

"Nah, not at all!" She dismissed my argument right away. "Who told you that? Where is this rule written?"

"But isn't that obvious?"

"Life is too complex, Paarth. Understand this, and empathize with people. You think good things aren't happening to you, that's why you eventually grow into a certain kind of a bad person. But when it comes to judging people, looking into why they behave in a certain manner that is beyond your understanding, this is the first thing we forget to apply."

"You mean to say that there must be something that my father went through that made him this hard piece of rock who shies away from showing affection to his child?" I asked.

"Even if nothing ever happened, and you choose to believe this explanation, it will not stop you from loving him. It will not fill you with the negative thoughts that make you seem so ignorant and unloving. Eventually, one day, your consistent exhibition of love for him will melt him and transform him into the person that you have so long craved for."

I pondered over it for a while. I didn't want to admit it so easily, as it hurt my ego, but she sounded right. Absolutely right! My soul stood convinced. I was left with no justification to save my point of view. I began to question my own role as a son. Did I really do what was right? Did I perform my duty the way it was required of me?

What she said, if I implemented that, at least it would save me from the negativity that made me hate him. He was my father, and I wanted to tell him that I wanted him to be proud of me. I further felt sorry about my rude behaviour for all the years.

"You can make people think. You know that, Miss Relationship Expert?" I finally smiled, and looked at her with appreciation.

"But being a writer, I believe you have to think this way. Otherwise, with what you write, how would you ever be able to change lives of people?"

I was lost in her words again. They made me think once more. Here was a girl who had more faith in me than even I had. Here was someone who was giving me worth, more than I thought I deserved. Other than her faith in me, I admitted to myself that this was a marvellous session of counselling.

"I wish I can always have you by my side, to guide me. I am sure you will make me a better human being."

"Now the first step in making you a better person is, the moment you reach home, you are clicking a photo with your dad."

"This is a little tough, if you ask me to do it by today itself. That is asking for too much on day one of the session," I said.

"I am sure you are a very tough man," she said, and we laughed it off.

Since it was getting darker, we both decided to start walking. We eventually ended up jogging to the cafeteria, and grabbing a milkshake each. It was a pleasant evening, so all the seats were occupied, and we had to stand in a corner. I noticed after a while that the usual chitter chatter was dying down, and although the place was still full, a peculiar silence engulfed the atmosphere. We noticed that everyone was looking at a father-son duo sitting on a table, almost in the middle of the seating area of the cafeteria.

The father being very old and weak, it was his son, who was feeding his father with his hands. Every time the father would cough or food particles would drop from his mouth, the son would keep his handkerchief before his mouth, and clean, with no sign of embarrassment. After they were done eating, the son helped his father to get up. He held him by the arm, to help him stand on his wobbling knees.

Everyone got up from their chairs and clapped for the son. That simple bond of love gave me a huge lesson. Sometimes, our parents need us to show more compassion than they are able to. Upasna smiled at me and her smile said it all. I was a little ashamed, but I felt it was important, as I had learnt something significant.

As soon as I entered my house, I stormed inside my parents' room. My father was sitting with the support of the bed head, with a quilt half wrapping him. My mother was giving him his medicines, the spoon containing the syrup almost having reached his mouth. I stopped her and carefully took the spoon from her.

"Let me give the medicine to Papa today," I said as lovingly as I could.

"I have thankfully seen this moment before dying," he said with great difficulty. "My son still remembers I am his father."

I looked at him with love, keeping the spoon down.

"We shall live such moments every day now," I said.

"Are you under the influence of some spirit or something?" Maa asked sceptically, not believing her eyes.

"Here, Mumma. Take this!" I said, pulling the phone out from my pocket. "Click a picture of me and papa. We don't even have a photo together."

She did not take the phone; instead, folded her hands asking, "Do you need something from us? This seems fishy."

"Not at all," I said, smiling. Then I gently put the phone in her hand. "You have to click the middle button, ok?"

I spread my left arm over my father's shoulder, giving a wide smile as my mother clicked our photo.

"One more," I said, as my mother drew close to show it to me.

She went back to take her position. I kissed my father on his cheek and my mother captured that rare moment. I called out to my mother to take my place then. I stood next to her and clicked a selfie of the three of us.

I looked at the photos, showed them to Maa and Papa also. They smiled! I was sure I had seen them happy like this after a long time. That's when I decided, I would gift something relevant to the three of us sometime soon. I left them in their room, telling them I would be back in some time. I came to my living space before leaving, and found my sister's photo.

Our family picture was certainly incomplete without her in it. I was sure that the photographer would be able to manage fitting in her face into the photo I had just clicked. After that, I headed out of the house, only to be back a few hours later, with a gift wrapped in a sparkling silver sheet.

As I was about to enter the room, my mother called me from behind. She asked me to come into the kitchen as she wanted to talk. My father had slept, she whispered, and also that it would be better to let him rest.

I entered the kitchen and stood before her.

"I hope Papa is doing fine," I asked, a little worried noticing the gloom on her face.

She nodded her head, raising her hand a bit. It indicated that there was nothing to worry about.

I took a sigh of relief.

"Your father was very touched today," she then said.

I smiled, thought for a while, and nodded my head in satisfaction.

"I know you don't like both of us," she said. "We have been like enemies who have opposed your ideas of life. We have never supported you in anything you have wanted to do."

"Not at all, Maa. What are you saying?" I immediately reacted, not even letting her complete what she was saying.

"Let me finish," she said

"I am sorry," I said, gesturing for her to carry on.

"I also admit we have been unnecessarily harsh on you. You are putting in your best effort to take our family forward, and we never appreciate you for a single thing you do. Unlike other kids, you never ask for anything from us. You never demand anything. You understand our condition so well. I don't even remember when was the last time you expressed a wish to buy clothes for yourself."

Tears rolled down my eyes now. I had been dying to hear words of empathy from my parents. Circumstances had been such that I craved for them, but never got to hear them. And today, when I did really hear them, I couldn't keep my emotions in check.

"But child, I want you to know something. Something that's important for you to be aware of," she continued. "Your father will never tell you this, so maybe I should." She completed the sentence hesitatingly. Since this conversation was long overdue and was finally happening, I coaxed her to say it.

"Say it, please Maa," I said, holding her hand.

"Don't let your father ever know that I told you this," she said, very emotionally.

"We know you are a dreamer, Paarth. And obviously, you had to be this way, for your father was the same."

I looked up surprised, because I knew nothing of this.

"He had big dreams too. Big ambitions that shaped his life. He loved the game of hockey, wanted to represent India, always. It was his love for the game, he feels, that kept him from giving you a life you deserve to live. He often blames himself for not listening to his father's advice of focusing on studies. He often goes down the memory lane, thinking of his past. And on days when he is overwhelmed, he wishes he could change his decisions of the past."

My mother was in tears. She was saying all that with a very heavy heart.

"His last match, when he was twenty-one, was quite an experience. Memories from that day are like fresh wounds in his heart. Despite doing everything in his might, destiny stabbed him, and stabbed him the deepest. The hard work he had put in, the passion he had shown, the time he had invested, the sacrifices he had made – everything failed him."

"What happened? Tell me," I said. "I want to know."

"Selections were going on for University Hockey Team. Those shortlisted fifteen players were going to participate in All India Inter University Hockey Tournament. Your father didn't have enough money to afford the jersey and shoes. He went inside the field in his slippers and vest on which he wrote his name and number with a sketch pen. Inside he knew his game was great, however, not having the necessary gear would not let him get through. People laughed at him. They booed at him. They labelled him a *bhikhari,* a beggar. And yet, he played his best, scoring two goals. Nevertheless, no one cared. The coach, the selectors, the sports staff, everyone ignored his name. Even your grandpa and grandmother didn't sympathize with him."

"Then?" I asked, almost in tears.

"He went into depression. He had given his whole life to the game, and his talent had been brutally ignored because he didn't have enough money to show off. He had a very tough time dealing with his emotions. After all, the dream he had nurtured since he was 3 had broken for no mistake of his."

She stopped for a while. I offered her a glass of water. She sipped in a little, and kept it on the shelf. Then she heaved a deep sigh and started again, "Your father doesn't want his only child to feel the same pain that he took a lifetime to come out of. He often says, it's easy to live without money, but it is very difficult to live with regrets, with unfulfilled desires that couldn't be completed because of situations out of your control. He is scared that his only son talks of dreams with passion like he used to show in his young days; he is scared that somehow, you might end up facing a similar outcome. He doesn't want history to repeat itself. He wishes a smooth and a comfortable life for you."

It broke my heart to hear this. Here was a man fighting his own self to give me a life I craved, and I had been so selfish all along. "I am so sorry I have been misunderstanding you both. I am sorry, Maa. I am sorry," I cried hugging her tight.

"All this while, he has been maintaining distance with you because he knows you are not wrong. So what is the point of stopping you? But at the same time, he understands how the real world works."

Saying that, my mother left the kitchen in tears. I had no answer that I could give to myself. Didn't have the courage to look into my own eyes. I couldn't understand how to go to my father and apologize for taking his gestures in the wrong way all along. I had judged him without ever trying to know his side of the story. Being his child, I thought, it was my fundamental right for him to accept me. Nonetheless, I so conveniently ignored that he would have wanted to be understood too.

Because of the way things had turned out, I had forgotten what all he had done for me till now. I was never grateful to realize the blessing that he was. I always underrated when he said he didn't want me to reduce to a mere taxi driver. I never considered his keeping his share of sweet in my plate as an act of love. I never thanked him when he wore old shoes that had begun to hurt his feet, and made sure I had a fresh pair.

Everything, I understood, that our parents do for us, can never be wrong. Yes, their experience of the world can be limited, no doubt, but their intentions can only be good. I decided, I will apologize to my father the next morning. I would tell him that there was nothing more important for me than him. His smile would be the mission of my life. Not for a single day more would my old man have to worry about anything.

I kept the gift safely behind the door of the kitchen and went inside my room. I finally looked at Upasna's text I had received an hour back.

Did my student finish his homework?

Not just the homework, he has mastered the complete syllabus.

Can you please explain? I didn't get you.

Thank you for enlightening me. My mother was in tears today. My father was very happy. I wish I had met you earlier. Thank you a million times.

I don't believe this!

I'll see you and explain everything. And, I'll forever be grateful to you. It's just because of you that I did what opened my parents to me.

I am happy that I could be of help.

Help is a small word, Upasna. It's a very small word. You have transformed things for me. You have changed my life from here. You will know when I share it with you. P.S. – I am not exaggerating at all.

Share them soon! Maybe tomorrow itself. I leave for Germany day after.

What? Are you kidding me?

Holidays are over. Time to leave. I'll be back during winters. For a longer period of time.

I did not reply to her last message. While I was happy to have learnt my father's intentions, I was disappointed to know she was leaving in just about two days, and I would, like always, have no one I felt so connected with.

Have you slept? Or are you ignoring me?

Upasna texted within a few minutes again.

I am not feeling too good. Will ping you tomorrow.

After hitting send, I switched my phone off.

THE FIRST THING I DID NEXT MORNING WAS PICKING UP THE GIFT from behind the kitchen door and heading towards my father's room. A thousand emotions that I wanted to convey started clouding my mind. I opened the door to his room and called out to him gently.

He did not respond. Maybe he was still sleeping. I called out louder. He did not respond again. I put my hand over his chest and very softly called him, sitting by his side.

"Papa."

I got no response. He had been on a lot of medication, and sometimes his sleep was very deep under their effect. His eyes were closed and his mouth a little open and still.

I called out louder, hoping he would wake up. No response again!

That's when panic set in. He had never been like this before. There was a lump in my throat, which I swallowed with great difficulty.

I called out louder, still he did not move! Doubts started raising their head in my mind.

I put my fingers right next to his nostrils, and then my hand on his chest to feel his heartbeat. I could sense nothing. I stood up in shock, breaking into tears immediately. Losing control over my footsteps, I fell back against the wall, and I held my head. I did not realize how hard I was crying till my mother stormed into the room from the kitchen, hearing me cry.

At the tender age of 18, I had lost my father. It was all the more vicious because my strained relationship with him had finally seen some hope. It was just a night ago that I had started to see that gap vanish from between us. And now, just as abruptly, he was no more.

The depth of my father's words hit me hard then – it's easy to live without money, but very difficult to live with regrets. I knew I was going to live with a burden all my life.

From that moment onwards, to cremation, to so many days that followed, I was filled with the same thoughts – why had I been so cruel to him? Why could I not let my anger go? Why could I not take control over my ego and take a step towards making things better with him?

My eyes had swollen because of crying. A week passed by, and I had barely eaten. Our house would be all dark during evenings and nights.

I remember hugging Kartik for hours and falling off to sleep like that, so many times. I was so heartbroken that I wanted to hold on to every loved one I was now left with. The lesson on my relationships had come to me the hardest possible way. Kartik would manage me and my state of mind most of the times. I could only wonder what I would have done without him. He was a rock solid support during that tough phase. For people who say it doesn't matter if they are hated by everyone, it is in such times that you get to understand the value of true relationships. Pain is a truth you cannot escape in relationships. The truer the relations you have, the more it helps you get through such times with ease. Leaving everything else, keeping aside his tasks and priorities, Kartik would sit by my side and soothe my pain.

THE MOURNING WENT ON FOR AROUND A MONTH. I WAS NOT holding up too well, and was managing my emotions and health disastrously. My body wasn't even a shadow of what I looked like a month before – lifeless face, swollen eyes and drooping shoulders of a man who had lost something most precious. It seemed as if I had been starving for ages.

Finding us running out of basic resources now, I had no choice but to act responsibly and head back to work. I had to hold myself together for my mother, Kartik explained to me like a brother, for the millionth time. She had lost her companion of so long, and she needed me to show strength to find it for her own self.

When I turned my phone on, pulling the door of the car open, finally about to leave for the taxi stand after a month, a notification flashed on it. It read *Upasna sent you 211 messages*.

I felt like a culprit now, having messed up things on another level too. It did not occur to me that she would be waiting to hear from me. I quickly opened my inbox and saw the whole list of messages. Upasna had been let down in a huge way. Her initial messages were for fixing our meeting. Then a couple of goodbye texts when she was about to board her flight, followed by updating that she had reached Germany, and finally demanding the reason I wasn't responding and why my phone was unreachable.

Wasting no time, I replied, informing her of my father's demise. I also added that I hadn't been in the right frame of mind since then, mentioning how everything had gone haywire. Within five minutes of the message getting delivered, she rang me up.

I was driving, and was currently crossing a traffic signal. Despite that, I went ahead and took her call. I wanted to hear her voice so desperately.

"Hello," I said in a very low tone.

"I am in deep agony, Paarth. I know words of sympathy cannot make up for your loss, but please hold yourself together. You are much needed," she said.

I could barely manage to speak.

"Paarth, are you listening?" she asked, very softly.

"Yeah," I replied with great difficulty. I could feel that she was also about to break down.

"I'll come soon and hug you tight. I am sorry for not being there with you at such a time," she said.

"Thank you for calling. It means a lot," I said.

"Please take care of yourself. I'll get back to you in some time," she said.

"Sure," was all I could say.

I sensed immense love and care in her voice. There was no element of formality. She sounded truly protective and worried. That made me feel slightly better. I had lost my father at a crucial stage in life. However, her few words of concern discounted on the pain I was going through.

In the afternoon, while inside the car, I dozed off to sleep. There were no passengers and I did not want to go back home yet. I woke up with a jolt to my phone ringing in my shirt pocket. It was Upasna again, insisting on making a video call. I declined politely. I didn't want her to see my swollen eyes, my upset face. She was adamant though, and had to have me over it. I was left with little choice.

Upasna looked like magic. Her expression was of deep pain, with her hands covering her mouth. As she moved the phone a little away, I noticed her purple jacket and diamond earrings. She looked very fresh.

"I guess it's time to go for class?" I said.

"I have about half an hour before I leave," she said.

She then inquired what went about all of a sudden, and it bomb-shelled her to the core. I also informed her about the first and last photographs I had taken with my father, and his story that my mother had narrated to me that evening. She deserved a big thanks for insisting on my settling things down with my family, and I showed gratitude to her for getting me a token of memory with them, which otherwise would have pinched me forever.

Seeing me in tears and unable to carry on, she closed the topic then and there. She tried to take my mind off the pain by cracking jokes and showing her golden retriever to me. The dog displayed a kindly expression. It appeared he had understood the heaviness of the situation and was trying to be as kind as possible. She introduced me to her American roommate Kristie who had just entered. Her hello was like a sugar-coated candy.

She walked to the balcony then, where she could talk to me in private. The dog followed her.

"How is aunty? Is she doing fine?" she asked.

"A little better now, but not much improvement," I said.

"You turned your phone on today?" she asked.

"Yes, I had no clue what was going on around me," I said. "The loss is so big; I was shaken to the core."

"Take your time. And drive very carefully," she said. "Don't let any negative thoughts come to your mind while on the road. You must understand that a strained relationship with your family was not your fault. Sometimes it's the circumstances too, and you have to stop blaming yourself about it."

"Hmm. I wish I get to be on the road," I said.

"What is that supposed to mean?" she asked, crinkling her nose in confusion.

She looked so cute like that, so I smiled and told her, "No work today. I have come after a month and I need money," I said. "We are left with like seventeen hundred rupees at home and there's nothing else saved up too. I wonder if I will earn enough for even the fuel or not."

"Send me your bank account details. Let me help you," she promptly said.

I realized my confessing like that could have led her to think I was subtly asking for help. I quickly gathered my thoughts and told her, "Please, you don't have to take this on you. I'll sort it out myself."

She insisted, trying her best to convince me. She even offered money as loan that I could repay any time. Since I wasn't sure if I would be able to return it, I had to be firm in saying no and humbly steering the conversation to something else.

But when had she given up so easily. After a minute's thought, she said, "What if I get you work? Would that be fine?" she asked.

"And how would you do that?" I asked.

"We have many Indians here in Germany. Their families come to pick them up from the Delhi Airport and back. Sometimes even our friends come and visit India. They need to have a taxi. Why don't you drive them around?"

"But how will you make that happen? Is it that easy for you?" I asked, surprised.

"I just have to drop your number in our group chat boxes. I am sure something will come."

"I'll be really thankful if you can do that," I said

Wasting no time, she shared my number, and it took no more than a week to start seeing a positive result. My taxi was booked by a person named Markus Schmidt who was coming from Munich. He and his mother wanted to see the Kitchen of the World. I didn't understand what place he was talking about at first, and where in Punjab it was. How would I take them there otherwise! Later on, I figured out, he was talking about the *langar* at the Golden Temple in Amritsar. It is actually one of the biggest kitchens in the world, feeding more than a lakh people every single day.

On the night that Schmidt and his mother were to arrive, I held up at the Delhi Airport. I used a cardboard with his name written on it. I kept waiting, and looking at my watch. It was now quite late. I could not understand how to respond to the situation. My heart sank, checking that the flight had landed long ago, and my heart told me I had been fooled. My intuition was most certainly right. I waited there for one extra hour, hoping against hope. No one turned up.

I wondered if I should check with Upasna. If she could give me any clue about these people... but what would be the use. She would feel guilty that I had wasted my time and fuel to reach the airport to not find the passengers who had come to me by her reference. And honestly, it wasn't her fault.

The moment I turned my back and began walking, a hand came and tapped my shoulder. I thought they had finally come. So I turned around, a flash of happiness inside me. It wasn't them though. It was Upasna Sharma standing right in front of me. Her arms open. I was astonished, and blown away.

"How on earth is this possible?" I muttered.

I rubbed my eyes in disbelief, almost sure I was hallucinating. She smiled wider at my antic, and came forward and hugged me tight. I closed my arms around her, locking her in an embrace I was dying for. My eyes closed on their own, and I felt so peaceful. So safe. All my tensions, my frustrations, my fears, my pain were flushed out. I felt as if everything was fine now. The bad times were gone.

A couple of people passing by hooted at seeing us locked in an embrace. All of a sudden, I realized I was standing at a public place. Both of us moved a step back and looked into each other's eyes very shyly.

"Where did you turn up from?" I asked

"When someone I so earnestly admire is down, how can I leave him alone?" she said.

"So that Markus, his mother, the visit to Golden Temple was a trick to call me here?" I asked.

"Of course, otherwise your selflessness would have never made this meeting possible," she said.

I looked down behind her, on her sides and everywhere around. "And where is your luggage?" I asked. There was only a Zara paper bag in her hand

"Umm, I am flying back in a few hours. I got my return tickets."

"You mean, you came here to see me? That's it?"

"... You can say that," she said.

"But why? Who am I to you?" I said. It was too much for me to see such care in someone I had barely known.

She clenched her fists tight, feeling scared of my reaction.

"You are... important. A very good writer also. I am a huge fan," she said, nervously.

"You do know what you are saying is not convincing at all, right?" I said.

"Dump your questions, na. I have a little time here. Let's go and have coffee together," she said.

"You have to explain this, Upasna. This is not a film going on. We aren't trying to give a feel good factor to some audience. This is life! This is reality! And this is cliché! You fly here from some country that must be two days far."

"Ten hours," she corrected me.

"Okay, ten hours far," I continued. "It's terribly long. You don't do it for a friend. Not as a fan either. Particularly when I am not even successful yet."

"Why do you have to shout?" she said.

I realized my voice had gone a notch higher in volume because of the whole adrenaline rush. "I am not shouting. I just spoke it too fast, I am sorry," I said.

She made a baby like face, looking down, as if I had scolded her.

"Okay listen," I further continued. "You don't have to answer anything. When do you have to go, tell me?"

She didn't reply, but just kept looking at her shoes.

"When do you have to go, dear?" I asked lovingly.

"In about an hour from now," she said, finally looking up at me.

"Did you have something to eat?" I asked.

"Food is life." She brimmed.

"And you are never late with it, right?" I too smiled.

"You remember that! Wonderful."

We sat inside a coffee shop for nearly fifty minutes. We didn't say anything for so long. I was scared to speak. She was confused. Our eyes would meet for a while. We would smile, and glare away. It almost seemed as if she wanted me to strike a conversation. On the other hand, I wanted her to do so. After an unexpected hug, this seemed all the more awkward. May be we weren't able to face each other after the impact of that moment was over. Or maybe, we wanted to confess the feelings we had for each other, but were apprehensive.

She waved her hand in goodbye before leaving. Quite apparently, we were enforcing extra control over our bodies. It was clearly written in her eyes that she was helpless and that she didn't want to go. My eyes were playing a double game. They were stopping her. At the same time, asking her to go.

I could feel her fragrance on my clothes. We kept looking at each other till she vanished from my sight.

Just a few seconds before leaving, she had handed her Zara paper bag to me. There was a leather jacket inside. When I took that jacket out and wore it, I realized there was something poking out of the right inner pocket, which was also heavy. I buried my hand inside to check and pulled the thing out. It was a letter and a bundle of five hundred rupee notes.

I unfolded the letter and saw the beautiful handwriting. It read:

Dear Paarth,

I have never said this to anyone before and I don't think I am ever going to say this to anyone again. I LOVE YOU.

Please don't think I am mistaking sympathy for love. Don't think you are in a tough phase and since I am very emotional, I am unable to see you going through it and hence have lost my mind.

I was in love with you the moment I had finished reading your book. The purity of your thoughts, the simplicity of your words and the magic of your story, everything took over me. I tried finding you out everywhere possible and even reached out to your publisher. He refused to share your number, but gave me your email id on which I wrote several emails.

But I guess, you didn't check them ever or you would have known me by now as your number one fan.

I don't know how crazy I am sounding to you as we have barely met twice. But all I can say is, I love you.

And trust me, I am not helping a person in need; I am helping someone I am madly in love with. Someone who I think is also in love with me.

In case he is not, please feel free to credit back my money in the account number mentioned below. I promise I will never bother you again after that. I swear I will never talk to you after that.

Upasna
Account number: 5543123487650937654
IFSC code: RRSS0000999

I hadn't encountered anything so adorable in my life before. The letter was so profoundly written. Everything was so neatly explained. She came travelling six thousand kilometres and back to pull me out of my trouble. What more could I ask for! I felt loved and important like never before. I couldn't help but smile in happiness, standing where she had left me. I was very sure she belonged to me. That she was like a part of my soul.

My sheer faith that one day my life would change for good had proven right. That's how god helps us, isn't it? Through people that he sends over to us.

I slapped my palm on my forehead, thinking of all the emails she must have sent to me. How could I be so stupid to forget the password to the email id I had mentioned in my book and never look at it again!

I laughed, stretching my vision to the point where Upasna had finally vanished from my sight. "And they say true love doesn't exist. Stupid people," I mumbled.

I took my phone out and texted Upasna.

Dear Upasna,

I am happy to inform you that your money has been accepted in the form of interest free loan. You have touched the deepest corner of my heart today. I still can't believe if this is some dream, or was this for real? Never expected someone to help me in this extraordinary manner.

I won't thank you by using the very traditional phrase. I'll do it by loving you all my life. It is also very important for you to know, that it's not your gesture due to which I say this. Or because I feel obliged or whatever.

Truth is, the moment I saw you for the first time, you were my destination. I am sure you remember the cardboard slipping out of my hands and hitting the man standing next to me. It was all your fault. I was so lost in your eyes that I went completely numb.

Having said that, whenever you find the entire world against you, turn and you shall have me standing there, right beside you. I feel so stupid to learn that I never read your emails. Though it was our fortune to meet, I guess this could have started long before. I am sorry you had to wait.

I LOVE YOU! ALWAYS WILL! I PROMISE!

Paarth

"Number one person in your life, huh? Number one?" Kartik said, staring at me angrily, his hands folded.

I was sitting inside his shop on a stool, while he was across at the counter on the wooden board. There was a table between us. It was late in the evening and I had gone to meet him. I discussed the events from last evening. Kartik, after hearing everything, was shattered and heartbroken.

He mocked a long cry falling on the floor, saying he could not believe that someone could fall in love with me, while he was still single. In addition to that, when out of pure emotions I ended up saying that she was the number one person in my life, he got back in his place and began to sing *'Achha sila diya tune mere pyar kaa, yaar ne hi loot liya ghar yaar kaa!'*

"Because she gave you fifty thousand rupees, she is the number one person. I gave only ten thousand, why would I be respected?"

"But you gave stolen money. She must have toiled hard over the weekends, earned this giving her sweat and blood."

"Motherfucker, her father must be a loot. No one can give their fucking hard-earned money to a selfish man like you. No one!"

"Why are you so jealous of me? I don't understand," I said.

"Listen, you driver…," he said, pointing a finger at me.

"Cum writer," I interrupted

"Writer, my ass! A beggar like you should be made to dance nude at India Gate."

He went on and on and on. "I don't understand this. With the sort of face you have, no one would throw their shit on it, and here comes a beautiful girl, who not only falls for you, but also starts giving you a heavy pocket money. Strange!"

"This is called Karma, my friend," I said.

"This is called Kalyug, you ass," he countered.

"I am telling you, you will not be able to digest this money… Na!"

"Ok, what would you like to have now? It's on me," I said.

"I can't eat out of an innocent girl's money. I have some ethics to follow. Some principles to stand by."

"A man who enters every wedding in the city for free food and booze shouldn't be talking of principles," I commented.

He made an angry face.

"Tell me… Come on!" I said.

His drama continued for a while. I kept doing my job of pushing him.

"Miller. Two bottles," he finally said. "And snacks separately."

"Done!" I said, smiling at him.

"Take in writing from me, god will never forgive you." He again started cribbing, getting up to close the shop for the day. "This is pure injustice to a great soul. Pure injustice!"

Standing by my words, I took Kartik out. Sponsored by me, indirectly by Upasna, we walked our distance to ISBT 43. Adjacent to a petrol pump, there was a narrow road with a huge ground on its left side. By the side of it, stood 4-5 small vendors who were famous for omelettes and Maggi. A tavern from which we purchased bottles of beer was also close by. We ordered two bread omelettes of three eggs each, and stood a little far in the ground where the last ray of light reached.

"By the way, how did you do this?" Kartik asked, sipping his beer.

"Did what?" I asked, holding the other bottle that he would drink.

"Trapped an innocent girl in your vicious web?" he said.

"Come on! You know me better than that! And anyway, I didn't apply any formula or did anything knowingly," I said. "It was meant to happen, so it did."

"Why then has it never happened with me?" he asked.

"Because it's not meant to happen?" I said, raising my eyebrows with a naughty smile playing on my lips.

He pulled the bottle away from his lips. "Listen, I am already in extreme pain. Any more insult and I'll smash this on your head," he said.

I laughed.

"Show me her photo," he commanded next.

"Find her on Facebook. Her name is Upasna Sharma. I don't have her photo yet. I video call her generally," I told him.

He pulled his phone out and typed her name in the application. Several profiles flashed. The top profile was hers. He opened the profile and then her display photo. He looked at the photo and then me. Then he looked at the photo again, and then at me again. He did this for some seven to eight times, and mocked having a heart stroke and difficulty in breathing, like he was choking.

"She said yes to you?"

"Yes!"

He then gulped the rest of the bottle in one go and smashed it on the ground. He snatched the other bottle from my hand and opened it with his teeth, spitting the straw on my face.

"Here it comes!" I said as I saw a small boy of eleven or twelve years bringing our omelettes in disposable plates.

"Give this in the hands of this moron," Kartik said to him.

I held them in both hands, trying hard to control my laughter.

"You will not take even a single bite from these. You don't deserve to eat. You should starve to death," he said.

"Sure, sir," I said.

He kept sipping his beer, taking one bite of the omelette after another, looking sternly at me all the while. When about thirty percent of the food remained, he told me, "You eat this, driver!"

I dug into it immediately, laughing in bits over his dramatic reaction.

"Let me tell you something," he said, when I almost finished eating. "I'll also become a writer."

I almost choked on the food I was eating. After I had finished coughing chunks of it out in shock, I asked him, "What did you just say? Pardon me please."

"I have decided, I'll also become a writer."

"Spell writer. Can you kindly spell writer?" I asked.

He threw the bottle to his left in style. "Okay," he said, stretching his arms. "Let me spell it for you, driver."

He looked at me straight in the eyes, opened his mouth to speak, my eyes fixed on it, all ready to make fun of him. Out of nowhere, he showed me his middle finger.

"This is what I am going to give to you for now," he said, with some sheer determination, and I ran as fast as I could, knowing what he was going to do.

He ran after me, laughing. I ran faster. But more than the two of us, time ran. The fastest.

Four Years Later

I was twenty-two years of age, and Upasna a beautiful girl of 26. And my dear Kartik... well, he was still frustrated.

Ours panned out to be a near perfect relationship. In the time that went by, Upasna completed her education from Germany and returned to India, taking a job in an MNC. Her initial plans were of having a well-settled life in America or Europe. However, for us, she decided to stay close, making me her priority. For the same reason, she left lucrative packages in NCR region and in south India, and took what she got in Chandigarh. Even her family was surprised at what she was doing, but their happiness of having their daughter close by didn't lead to much suspicion.

To cut the long story short, whenever a sacrifice was required from one of us, she took the first step. She understood my state really well and knew time wasn't in my favour, yet.

Her empathy was unbelievable. Not for a second did she ever let me feel that she had better opportunities which she was missing out on. Upasna had further closed down on all the walls to make me feel secure about her. Her life was limited to her work, family and me.

On the other hand, there wasn't any incredible change in my life in all those years. My struggle for work and money still existed on the same level. The manuscript I had written was rejected by every publishing house in the country, with many of them stating that it wasn't commercially viable. On some days I did think of going the way I went with my first book.

But paying a publisher, I had understood, was more of a trap for budding authors. If you aren't good enough according to them and they aren't interested in promoting you, they won't publish you traditionally. Meaning thereby, I had to be a better proposition. Write a better manuscript (which I had already started working on and reached the middle of) and come up with an interesting marketing plan.

This manuscript, the third book I was officially writing, I had for now called it *The Man Called Happiness*. I was working really hard on it. Upasna, after her office hours, would devote her time reading it, giving me regular feedback. On some days when I would be extremely busy, Upasna would ask me how I was thinking on extending the plot further and would herself write for me and send it over.

Those days, she was under heavy stress. It isn't unusual for an Indian family to start looking for suitable matches for their girls the moment they finish their education. Upasna was almost twenty-six, and her relatives, friends and almost everyone had prying eyes on her. Meet them after a few days and they would fire questions at you: "When are you getting married? Why are you not getting married? What are you waiting for? Have you been rejected? Blah blah blah." Their behaviour would sometimes make you wonder if they were getting something out of your marriage too, a commission or something.

A plethora of marriage proposals were being brought to her by her parents, by relatives, etc. The cycle was going on and the motives were to see Upasna getting hitched at the earliest. She had declined over twenty proposals in a month and her family had finally asked if she was seeing someone. She, of course, couldn't answer in a yes as I wasn't doing very well in my career. What could she have said! I was trying my best to make things easy on her. I assured her I would at the soonest finish my work, get it published, enabling her to share something about our relationship with her family.

But then, irrespective of the intensity of pressure or the fear that lay in the unpredictability of tomorrow, I didn't want to lose out on the fun we were going to have on our trip to Haridwar. Upasna's college friend Kristie and Ugo Nourry, Kristie's husband, had come to visit the holy place. It was astounding for me to see both of them carrying a copy of the *Bhagavad Gita* when they met us on arrival at the airport.

I was in the driving seat with Upasna next to me. In the back sat the beautiful and generous foreign couple. We were around eight kilometres away from our destination on NH334 and had been discussing significance of god and religion all our way.

"Religion is meant for the purity and enlightenment of the soul," Kristie commented.

"But over here, in India, they say religion makes people helpless or it turns them into terrorists," I said.

"Elbow people have lost their mind. They are no longer connected to their roots," Kristie said.

"Elbow people?" I asked.

Upasna looked back at her friends, and the three of them burst into laughter.

"I am sure Upasna wouldn't have told you, did you Upasna?" Ugo said.

I looked at Upasna for a second. "What's that?" I wondered.

"In Germany, we refer to Indians as elbow people," Kristie said. "You cannot expect them to patiently wait in line. They've got to move ahead, pushing others using their elbows. Never caring about discipline or being courteous."

"Goodness me! Have we earned such a bad reputation? Upasna, are you the same?"

"Not me, Paarth. She is talking about the majority of us."

"But Kristie, why do you say we aren't connected to our roots anymore?" I asked, looking at her through the rear view mirror.

"Because of this. Ting, ting, tiding!" Kristie said, lifting her copy of the *Bhagavad Gita*.

"Written two thousand years ago, still relevant as if it is made to solve the modern-day problems of human beings, you people have left this far behind. Ignored this for so long. What is supposed to be your truest treasure has been left behind so you can run after materialistic things! Don't you think it takes a stupid mindset to forget your heritage?"

I couldn't agree more.

"I hope we are not going to miss out on the Ganga Aarti, are we? That's the first thing I plan to see," Kristie asked leaning forward.

"Completely depends on the traffic. Though I think we are on time."

The knowledge and enthusiasm these two foreigners exuberated for rituals that we loved to miss out on was an eye-opener. There ought to be a great significance of what they wanted to experience. Each and every thing in their to-do list was what we considered boring and superstition.

"But Kristie, tell me..." I asked out of curiosity, "who told you about the Ganga Aarti?"

"My grandma lived in Rishikesh for fifteen years. She had become a monk. She often told us that the Ganga Aarti is one of the most spiritually uplifting and meditating experiences you can ever witness"

"Alright," I said, fascinated.

"Quite sure, you must have experienced Ganga Aarti like a thousand times," Ugo said.

I felt ashamed in confessing. "Not even once, my friend."

"I told you about elbow people," Kristie commented.

I looked at them in the rear view mirror and smiled.

THE VIEW AT HAR-KI-PAURI, WHICH IS REGARDED AS ONE OF THE most holy places in terms of spiritual significance, was majestic. It was indeed very fortunate for us to have reached on time. Upasna and Kristie took a dupatta to cover their heads like all other ladies had done. Ugo and I dawned a simple kurta pyjama, and carefully walked down to the ghat, holding the hand of our ladies.

The stairs were slippery, and were filled with people waiting for the aarti to begin with folded hands. The temple priests stood facing the river on banks on both the sides. Most of them wore a very light-coloured dhoti and covered the upper torsos with just a saffron cloth. With the sound of the conch shell, the priests began to chant mantras and hymns in praise of river Ganga, circling the lit brass lamps in a clockwise direction. People floated burning diyas on small cups made of dry leaves, making a wish.

The clanging bells, billowing flames, melody of the flowing river, and hundreds of devotees singing along with the priests and saints, was an experience of a kind. My soul felt at peace and the mind was soaked in devotion. It was like the most powerful soul cleansing experience one can ever get in the world.

Kristie and Upasna stepped forward, closer to the priest and said something in his ear. The priest took a step back and was generous enough to let them hold the brass lamp. Both of them gestured at us to come nearer. First, Ugo and Kristie together performed the ritual. Then, Upasna and I followed. I took moments out to look at Upasna in between. Her eyes were fixed on our hands and her mild smile spoke volumes of the depths of our love. Then, she looked at me with compassion. Our eyes stayed on each other what seemed like forever. We knew exactly what we were wishing for.

After the aarti was done, Ugo and Kristie went to explore the market, while both of us sat in silence on the stairs. Most people around us had left by now. Upasna held my hand and kept her head on my shoulder, watching the river flow.

"It is so peaceful here." she muttered, throwing a gaze at the clear night sky.

"I think I'll keep coming back to this place. It has the power to purify a person from within. I have never experienced such an enlightening event before," I said.

"Kristie knows about it more than we do, despite her roots and all the distance. We have let our heritage down," Upasna said.

"For sure! When people like you will leave India and think of an American PR, this is bound to happen," I said seriously, but Upasna understood I was teasing her.

She punched me in the stomach lightly.

I laughed bending away. "I said the truth, you see. We don't need people like you anymore."

"As if you have devoted your life in the service of Maa Ganga," she said.

"I plan to spend it in the service of my love, Upasna aunty," I said, winking.

"It still seems a thing from yesterday when we met. The time has literally flown off," I said

"We must be proud of ourselves. We have been able to manage a long distance relationship," she said.

"Well, the next challenge awaiting is how long it goes from here," I said.

"You don't have to worry. We will reap what we intend to get from this bond of ours."

"What do you intend to get?" I asked straight, wanting to hear something good.

"First of all, two beautiful kids who look like both of us. Secondly, I want to grow old with you."

"I can quite grant your second wish. For the first one, I think I am too young. I don't want kids right after marriage. Even if you ask for that five years down the line, I will have to think about it."

She smiled and held my arm tighter.

"Don't worry, darling! It will only take a few sexy moves before I get you into doing my bidding, and have what I want," she said seductively.

I smiled at her, intrigued.

I held her hand in mine and said with fond love, "There is still a long way to go for all this. First, let me prove my worth. I don't think with what I have now, I can give you a fraction of what you are used to living with."

"It really doesn't matter what you own in terms of material wealth. Ultimately, you have to love the person and not the digits of their bank balance."

"With time, things change. People start being something they are not. Or maybe something that they must be in order to be happy. What if somehow you begin to feel I was a wrong decision?"

"In case of that happening, you have the license to think this wasn't love. A phase of attraction that ended like all other relationships do."

I nodded my head.

"But hey, our affection has lasted long enough. It can't be attraction, right? I have compared our metrics of love to a mother-child bond. We have passed with flying colors, I am happy to share." Upasna beamed with delight.

"Your faith makes me stronger and more determined each day. I take new resolutions for the confidence you have in me. I might have given up the dream I am chasing if I didn't have you by my side. After failing this many times, anyone would believe they aren't good enough. But your presence makes me believe I am close. So I have my absolute good and valid reasons of loving you."

"I don't know why you have this sweet yet stupid habit of underrating your efforts and gestures."

"Only if I had done something worth being proud of," I said honestly.

"It isn't easy for anyone to accept a PCOS patient, Paarth. Trust me! It isn't easy at all. My parents were so concerned of this situation that they decided they would never let this out in the family they would marry me in. You saved me from the wrath of that lie. I shuddered to think what would have happened when the truth came out to the people my family decided to cheat on."

"What's the big deal about PCOS anyway, Upasna? It's a problem, so what?! So many of us have so many problems," I said casually, trying to tell her it was no big deal.

"Mr Paarth! Polycystic Ovary Syndrome is a hormonal disorder causing enlarged ovaries with small cysts on the outer edges. You know that treatment can help, but this condition can't be cured. And that is a big deal for a lot of people, especially older women in the family who think it is some sort of a hindrance to their lineage growing."

"What if I was in your place and diagnosed with something like that, Upasna? Would you leave me then?" I wanted her to realize through her answer, which I was sure of, that what I had done wasn't anything special. That's the first responsibility you naturally take for someone you love. You can't hold and leave someone's hand based on how their life is running. A mother never does that. A father never does that. If their child is suffering, they don't abort their relationship with them and walk off and begin afresh being parents to new kids. Because that's not what love is. You hold a hand, once and for all. Irrespective of what they will be able to offer.

"A year before, when I was diagnosed with it, I thought you would leave me. It made sense as well. I had even made up my mind, knowing it was going to be the right decision for you, and that you must move on."

I held Upasna tighter, kissing the side of her forehead, sensing the heaviness in her voice. The reason behind her complex must have stemmed from learning how negatively her body could transform due to PCOS. After all, more than half of women with PCOS have diabetes or pre-diabetes before the age of 40. It can also lead to high blood pressure, higher cholesterol and obesity. There is even a risk of developing cancer of the lining of the uterus or womb.

I didn't care about what could possibly go wrong with her. That was simply not under anyone's control. Nevertheless, what I could best do was make her realise she was good, as she was. That nothing around her would ever change. I grew more affectionate towards her. Yes, I can't deny, the first thing that intrigued me about her was her beauty. However, the more time I spent time with her, the more I fell in love with who she was. The values she had. The kindness in her heart. The purity in her beliefs.

I was prepared to see her physically changing over a period of time. Had it not been PCOS, age would have overtaken. All of us would look different in some years from now anyway. We are young today. Proud of our looks and energy. But this is temporary. A matter of a few more years. Nothing different was going to happen to her. It's just that it would arrive for her a year or two earlier than its scheduled time.

She added, "I was actually thinking of encouraging you to break up with me. You were hell bent on staying. I thought you were being childish and immature. Filmy kind. Like how can I leave when you are in pain, I am your one true lover."

"We don't like suffering, Upasna. All of us want to resist it. It causes sadness and pain. It pushes us in isolation. One by one, everyone we have any kind of expectations from, leaves.

So does hope sometimes. Still, in one way or the other, we all will continue to suffer. We can't help but acknowledge it. That's how life works."

"When we can clearly see a storm coming our way, we must step back and run away."

"When you see your loved one stuck in that storm, you walk towards it, extending your hand to your loved one. You only care about saving them, even if it has to come at your cost."

"This storm isn't meant for you, Paarth!"

"Everything was meant for us the moment we decided to be together."

"What if someday, in anger, you blame me for missing opportunities that you might have to?"

"If missed because of you, they can't be opportunities."

AT AROUND MIDNIGHT, THE FOUR OF US MET IN THE HOTEL. UGO and Kristie had booked one large room in a three-star accommodation. The staff upon our request had arranged for two mattresses for some extra bucks on the floor, on which Upasna and I lay down to sleep. It was fairly comfortable, but there was no natural light. As we switched the tubes off, it was completely dark inside.

"Do you know how this city of Haridwar came into existence?" Kristie asked out of nowhere.

"You've got to stop testing my knowledge, Kristie, or your husband isn't going back with his wife," I answered in a lazy yet serious tone.

Upasna and Ugo chuckled.

"According to Hindu mythology, the city was created when a drop of nectar spilled over from *kundalini* which was being carried by the celestial bird Garuda after Samudra Manthan." Kristie showed off some knowledge and superiority.

I took the pillow from underneath my head, turned sideways and kept it on my ear. This mainly summed up our entire Haridwar journey. Prominently highlighted by our walk in the narrow lanes of the city bazars and Kristie's enthusiasm and curiosity for history and culture of Haridwar, for which she had been nudging me as if I were her tour guide, our Haridwar trip was one memorable stay.

We visited the Mansa Devi temple on top of a steep hill by a rope car. One can reach there by trek too if they can afford some extra time and are looking to challenge notorious monkeys on the way, who can snatch away almost anything from you within a fraction of a second.

Inside the temple, there was aggressive commercialism by priests who were bent upon making people get *puja* done from them. They were like irritating salesmen who should better be left ignored. To be honest, I personally felt ashamed of the way they were jumping on people with their packages of prayers. Ugo's and Kristie's expressions were a must watch. Both of them seemed blown away by their greed. One as an Indian would feel like shooting down all such morons who made religion look like a business.

Next, we visited Ram Sita Ashram, famous mainly for its peace and order. The place was named after a monk who is believed to have survived only on milk. It redeemed India's image before Ugo and Kristie, I was sure. The priests there were pure saints. They only blessed people with *prasad* and chanted mantras; that's it! Neither did they ask for money, nor did they jump on visitors. They were completely into their prayers.

Kristie added to our knowledge bank in the Ram Temple there. Enthralled by the thirty feet high statues of Ram Parivar and several other small idols of Hindu gods that had been so neatly maintained, she told us why any blessing or curse from neuter gender was given high significance in Hindu religion. It was interesting to learn that it was Lord Rama who had blessed them with that power when he found them waiting for him for fourteen years on his return to Ayodhya after his exile.

Bharat Mata Mandir, Vaishno Devi Temple, Patanjali Yog Peeth, Sapt Rishi Ashram and Chilla Wildlife Sanctuary were other beautiful places that we enjoyed seeing. There were several other sites we looked forward to, but Ugo and Kristie hadn't managed a long stay. They were to return to Germany as it was the end of their short holiday. They were an amazing couple. Not only did they have some extensive knowledge about Hindu culture, which was way more than mine and Upasna's put together, they were also very simple and sober in their conduct. I had a very solid perception about people from the West that they were fussy. My meeting with these people was a different experience altogether.

I vividly remember when Kristie and Ugo were about to leave and the former had hugged me tight, I was standing frozen. I had never hugged a girl except Upasna and I didn't know how to hug a girl who was supposed to be just a friend, with her husband standing right before your eyes. If you think of doing that to an Indian girl, you can surely expect bloodshed. My mind had no clue of whether to wrap my arms around her, or just stay where I was. She, on the other hand, was rubbing my back, telling me to meet again soon and get some classes on Hindu culture.

Ugo bade us goodbye, telling us to get married so that they could come back to India sooner. I very strongly told him that it was not going to happen for at least five years. Five years was a minimum period I was going to give myself to settle down, earn myself a name before taking Upasna's responsibility.

That being said, when have things moved as per plan in life? They choose to take their own course.

One of Upasna's acquaintances had seen her hugging me in Haridwar, and had informed her father about it. Upasna's father had immediately asked to meet me. Upasna had to tell him the entire truth about my age, family background and profession. Her father was baffled, of course. Particularly as a parent, when you have ensured your daughter's education in a country like Germany, you expect her to find some automobile engineer as a life partner, not a cab driver.

Thankfully though, her father was quite unlike a typical villain from Bollywood films. Ignoring his personal feelings about his daughter's choice, he said he would only take a call after meeting me. He kept this very private. Just to himself, and didn't even inform Upasna's mother about it.

I was called by her father when he was alone at home. I was a bundle of nerves, going stiff thinking how he would treat me. Or if he was planning to get me a nice thrashing from some hooligans. Kartik made fun of all this, labelling it as "child marriage". When I looked at my face in the mirror, which had beard only in patches, I thought he was right. He suggested me to meet Upasna's father without hesitation.

Mr Ram Kumar Sharma was very decent and polite in his looks. He was a complete epitome of his name. I sat before him in their large drawing room, with my head bowed, as if I was feeling sorry about everything.

He began with all the basic questions about my family, siblings, education and profession, the answers to which I am sure would have disappointed him. Then, he asked about how the relationship began – the first meeting and how things moved further. I truthfully answered all his queries.

Knowing almost all my twenty-two years of life, and that expression of despondence that loomed on his face since my first answer, he asked about my future plans. I told him I was looking to become a writer and that I was halfway through with my third book. I also shared with him the passion I exuberated for writing. He had a smile on his face listening to how I used to write everything in a pad and then go to a cyber café to type and get my work in print. For that, I arranged money by myself and never troubled my parents. I made paper bags out of newspapers and sold them to small shopkeepers.

Eventually, when all his questions came to an end, he went into a thoughtful silence. I don't know what he was thinking, but my breath was caught in my lungs for those few minutes. His glare was fixed on the floor. He seemed to be making calculations in his head. I sat there, more nervous than ever. It seemed he was about to announce the result of the toughest exam of my life. There was complete stillness engulfing us.

"I am sure you understand that this is a very tough situation for me," he finally spoke after fifteen minutes. "You are a nice boy. I respect the hardships you have faced and how you have come over them all. Not many can survive through all that and still have their dreams intact. You sure have some unique qualities."

"Thank you, sir," I said, feeling a little relaxed.

"What I should do now, I don't understand. I don't think I have ever said no for anything to my daughter. Nonetheless, I can't always let her take decisions when they hold the key to her future."

"I agree to what you say, sir. Whatever your decision may be, we'll respect that," I said.

"Look, I don't want to demean you, judging you on the basis of your bank balance. Even my father was a very poor man. He used to sell coal on a bicycle. Twenty years he did that. We have worked hard to reach where we are today," he said.

"Inspiring to hear that, sir," I said, honestly seeing hope in my future now. His was an inspiring story.

"I don't agree with your future plans, Paarth. What you are doing, the pace at which you are doing it, in my experience, I don't see great changes coming. Still, I'll give you 15 months from now. I am not going to say build a new home, collect a certain amount of money or anything like that. That's not possible for any human being. Therefore, let's talk practically and give you an achievable task. Make a good enough plan, and implement it. Every effort that you make, I want to see how smartly you do it, how efficiently you accomplish it. In case I am not satisfied, my son, you will have my hands folded and head in your feet to let my child out of this."

"Please don't embarrass me, sir. I will try to the best of my ability," I said.

"And that is all I want to check. Your ability. Your intention. Your courage," he said.

"Your father is such a genuine man," I said as Upasna escorted me out.

"I told you. You don't need to fear him," she said

"I wonder how success does not get into the head of such a rich man? Now I know why you are so kind and compassionate. All in the blood, huh!" I said.

She smiled. "We had a cook. He worked for us for close to ten years. Dad used to call him our Annapurna. Once I said to him when I was a child, that our family makes you work so much. Why don't you find a job somewhere else? Your burden will reduce and they will give you more money. He told me, maybe I'll get less work there and more money, but the respect your family gives me is unmatchable. They make me feel like an integral part of your family and everything here equally belongs to me. Not even for a single instance have I been rudely addressed or treated like a servant."

"Interesting! By the way, every word that your father said, his concern, his apprehensions... were all right," I said.

"So now what?" she asked. "How are you going to address his demand?"

"Writing a novel alone can't be enough. The outcome of it won't largely be in my hands. I'll have to think of something that can give me quick visible growth."

"Any clue what you are going to start with?"

"For now, all I know is, I am an uneducated man with no knowledge of anything but creative writing," I said.

"Which means?"

"Means... I don't know yet," I said.

"I am sorry to put you in this situation," she said. "Thankfully, you aren't taking it as a punishment."

"If ever I get to prove that I love you as much you love me, this is my only chance," I said.

I sat up the entire night, contemplating what possibly can help me through. My experience was quite limited to driving and writing. These were the only two things in the world that had made sense to me. Rest everything wasn't programmed for my brain. Or I should say, it was the other way round. My brain had never seen anything else.

I was getting some foolish ideas in between. But I knew they were better for jokes than implementation into work. I was tensed, yet determined. For an uneducated person to come up with a strong idea of change was next to impossible, it seemed. When my brain, which is god's amazing creation, gave up after some relentless hours of intense thinking, I resorted to the next best creation – Google.

I searched the phrase "How to become successful". In return, I got to read some shitty articles on self-discipline, conduct, motivation, soft skills and life hacks. There were unsuccessful philosophers with huge essays written on easy ways to find success. They irritated me to the core because they all said the same thing over and over, and I felt I was implementing more than that as a writer already.

Next, I entered a fresh phrase in the Google search bar - "Stories of richest people in the world". Most of the personalities that I initially read about had brought in radical change in the computer industry. Except for emails and MS Word, I knew nothing; not even playing a game. So I read about people who owned several luxurious brands, and then I stopped. It gave me a severe headache. I knew I could not conceive any such plan, as that wasn't me. I was reading through pages that never felt like my story. I was trying to be a part of things that never made sense to me.

My originality or my strength did not coincide with what these people ever were. Therefore, I explored something that was in line with my personality.

I thought of searching another phrase. I looked for "Famous stories of writers and actors".

I read about Agatha Christie, Tolkein, Joan Didion, Mario Puzo, JK Rowling and several others. These were all writers whose life story intrigued me, but did not fill me with fire or brought me a million-dollar idea. But, out of a strange interest, I kept on reading and exploring about more such people. Three hours flew by and every story had something unique to offer. Some real motivation to give. Finally, I bumped into the story that I wanted.

Back in the day, Stallone was a struggling actor in every definition. At some point, he got so broke that he stole his wife's jewellery and sold it. Things got so bad that he even ended up homeless. Yes, he slept at the New York bus station for three days. Unable to pay rent or afford food. His lowest point came when he tried to sell his dog at the liquor store to any stranger. He didn't have money to feed the dog anymore. He sold it at $25 only. He says he walked away crying.

Two weeks later, he saw a boxing match between Mohammed Ali and Chuck Wepner and that match gave him the inspiration to write the script for the famous movie, Rocky. *He wrote the script for twenty hours! He tried to sell it and got an offer for $125,000 for the script. But he had just* one condition. *He wanted* to star *in the movie. He wanted to be the* lead actor, Rocky himself.

The studio said no. They wanted a real star. They said he 'looked funny and talked funny". He left with his script. A few weeks later, the studio offered him $250,000 for the script. He refused. They even offered $350,000. He still refused. They wanted his movie, but not him. He said no. He had to be in that movie.

After a while, the studio agreed, gave him $35,000 for the script and let him star in it. The rest is history! The movie won Best Picture, Best Direction and Best Film Editing at the prestigious Oscar Awards. He was even nominated for best actor! The movie Rocky was even inducted into the American National Film Registry as one of the greatest movies ever.

And do you know the first thing he bought with the $35,000? The dog he sold. Yes, Stallone loved his dog so much that he stood at the liquor store for three days, waiting for the man he sold his dog to. And on the third day, he saw the man coming with the dog. Stallone explained why he had sold the dog and begged for the dog back. The man refused. Stallone offered him $100. The man refused. He offered him $500. And the guy refused. Yes, he refused even $1000. And, believe it or not, Stallone had to pay $15,000 for the same dog he had sold at $25! And he finally got his dog back.

And today, the same Stallone is one of the greatest movie stars who ever walked the earth! Being broke is bad. Really bad. Have you ever had a dream? A *wonderful dream? But you are too broke to implement it? Too tiny to do it? Too small to accomplish it? Life is tough. Opportunities will pass you by, just because you are a nobody.*

Whatever happens to you, keep dreaming. Even when they crush your hopes, keep dreaming. Even when they turn you away, keep dreaming. Even when they shut you down, keep dreaming.

Fight for your place in history. Fight for your glory. Never ever give up! Even if it means selling all your clothes and sleeping with the dogs! But as long as you are still alive, your story is not over. Keep your dreams and hope alive. Go, get it!

It gave me goosebumps. It gave me hope. It brought my spirit back, letting me know exactly what move I had to make. If Sylvester Stallone could write a script within a few hours and sell it on his conditions, I saw no reason why I could not sell my already written stories to filmmakers.

Writing a novel, getting it published, and making it successful was one long procedure. But, if I had a good story, it would only be about finding one single opportunity to make a producer listen to it. I realized that it was easier said than done, but then I had not even tried yet. I decided that my journey would start right away. It was 4.00 a.m. when I called up Kartik.

"Hello?" There was fear in his voice, as if anticipating something terrible.

"If one has to sell their story to a filmmaker, what is the process they must follow?" I asked.

"Motherfucker, at this hour? Have you gone mad?" He was shocked.

"Answer me!" I said, very serious.

"This is my time to sleep, not to entertain your ambitions," he said.

"You dare cut my call and I'll shove a stick up your ass," I warned.

"I am regretting your friendship, bitch. Now quickly bark out what you want."

"I need to sell my story to a filmmaker. What do I do?"

"First of all, go to Mumbai. Rest I'll tell you then," he said.

"Think practically. In my situation, can I?" I said.

"Yes, you cannot. So well, go to bed. Sleep!"

"How do I sell my story? Tell me!" I said.

"I can't bring Karan Johar or Aditya Chopra here to listen to you. Of course, you will have to shift to Mumbai and meet them in person."

"But don't you think Punjabi cinema is progressing by leaps and bounds; can't we approach these people?" I placed an idea forward.

"Punjabis only love comedy. You write cliché stuff. That rosy-posy, lovey-dovey, muaah-shuaah garbage. No one buys that here. Not the audience even," he said.

"You are wrong, mate. My perception on this differs. Eight out of the last ten Punjabi movies were comedies; one was action and one romance. The fact of the matter is that the romance movie garnered as much money as all comedy movies put together. Furthermore, we don't have an epic Punjabi love story that has been shown on silver screen yet. I feel this is an opportunity for me."

"My lord, if you already have such strong ideas and beliefs set in your head, what do you require from me? Validation?" He almost shouted.

"I don't know how you do this, but find me addresses of producers from Pollywood by evening. We need to start meeting them," I said.

"Excuse me? Who is this calling? Do I know you?" he said.

"If in twenty-four hours the job is not done, never show me your face again," I warned, and hung up.

CB

NEXT EVENING, I REACHED KARTIK'S SHOP. HE WAS STANDING WITH a notepad in one hand and a pen in the other, counting the stock in the shelves. I stood in the distance as his father was there too. I waited for uncle to move out, and once he did, I went to speak to Kartik.

Seeing me, he yelled, "Whatever you want, we don't sell, sir. Kindly get out. Get out!

I reached closer to him and asked calmly, "Done with the Shahrukh Khan in you?"

"I should rather be Amrish Puri. Which sensible person advised you to call me at 4 a.m.? If my father would have heard the phone ringing, he would have taken it away."

"That would have been good, isn't it?" I asked with a serious face.

"Yesterday, I made an account for myself on shaadi.com. And in a hurry, I forgot to turn the notifications off. Had he known about it, he would have torn me into two pieces."

"Who the hell makes an account on shaadi.com? At this age, you should have an account on Tinder."

"Listen, poster boy of child marriages, don't teach daddy. After complete devastation and hopelessness on Tinder, I have switched to shaadi.com."

"Not even a single girl responded to you on Tinder?" I asked. It was a new low for him also.

"It's not for innocent people actually," he said. "My kind of girls don't make an account on Tinder."

"Very smart way to justify failure, I must say. But who inspired you to have an account there?"

"To learn proper English and impress girls, I bought a novel. The protagonist got his girlfriend through this site only," he said excitedly, pretty sure his plan would work.

I looked at him with sheer sympathy. *What a desperate moron he was!*

"Did you do what I asked you to?" I asked, coming to the point.

"You remember Lala Babu Ram?"

"Lala Babu Ram?" I thought out loud.

"On Diwali, when we went to Sector 91 Mohali together? Remember? To pick boxes of biscuits from the godown of this short, stout man?"

"Umm?" I thought harder.

"You even drove his family to Vaishno Devi last year. I had booked you for him."

"Yes yes, I remember. Now I get that. Yes!"

"He owns a flat in Homeland, Mohali. He has rented that to Akash Singh, one of the most popular song writers in Punjabi music industry," he said. "They were showing on PTV channel that he is now writing a movie for Globe Punjab Productions."

"Putting this straight, you plan to reach Akash Singh for guidance through Lala Babu Ram?"

"Precisely."

"Let's make a move then."

"Right now?"

"No harm in checking. We still have a possibility of getting hold of him."

We quickly pulled down the shutter on Kartik's shop and headed to meet Lala Babu Ram. Though we were quite late, we were banking on Tricity's habit of seldom sleeping. I wanted to believe that this man we were going to meet would prove to be a savior. May be my old habit of finding positivity in everything was in action. I pressed the gas further to reach at the soonest.

Kartik warned me to mind my speed. The speedometer was clocking 100 plus kmph. I eased down as Chandigarh police has a reputation for giving rash drivers a tough time.

"Trying to make every second count, my friend," I said as an explanation. "I am sorry."

He, retorting to me, appreciated me for the dedication I was showing for Upasna. I felt ecstatic when he said he found my commitment for her no less than my passion for writing.

❤️

THE ENTIRE MARKET OF SECTOR 91 HAD SHUT DOWN. WE JUMPED out of the car to be doubly sure. A ray of light sneaked out through the tiny space between the floor and steel shutter of Lala Babu Ram's shop. We climbed the stairs to check. It wasn't locked, so we knocked.

"The shop has been shut down. Come tomorrow," came the voice from inside.

"Lala ji, it's me, Kartik. From Shyaam Confectionary."

"O my child! Pull the shutter up and come in."

VAT 69 and two soda bottles on the table, and a glass of wine in his hand was the scene that welcomed us. He had twirled his moustaches and looked like a living teddy bear. He stood up from his chair dwindling and tightly kissed both of us on our cheeks. He smelled bad. It was alcohol mixed with sweat; something that could get anyone to puke almost instantly.

"Sit down, my children, sit down!" he said.

"How are you, Lala ji?"

"Till now, I was good. Seeing both of you, now I am very good."

"Lala ji, we need a favour from you. If you can help us, we'll be extremely obliged."

"You need stock on credit, is it?"

"No, Lala ji. Actually, this friend of mine has written a story. It's a very good story, Lala ji. Super hit story you can say." Kartik was behaving like a news anchor, hyping everything. "You have that writer Akash Singh living in your flat in Homeland. If you can get us just five minutes of his time for us, it will be so kind."

"I would have been able to help you if you had approached me four months back."

"Why not now?" I asked.

"He is a very rich man now. He has moved into his own house. He is in very high demand throughout the industry. For one song he writes, he charges a minimum of seven lakhs. And now, he is also writing movies I've heard."

"Lala ji, we have come with great hope. If you can help us in any way, please do."

"You both are my son's age. I'll explain this to you in detail. No one becomes successful by taking guidance from successful people or by asking them to create a way. If you want to reach where Akash is today, build your own road."

"Lala ji, but…"

"Let me finish…. let me finish," he requested. "Do you think Akash became who he is because some writer guided him? No. I'll tell you how he struggled. He would sit outside producers' houses for hours, waiting for them to listen to him. Two years later, after requesting and begging, they decided to give him a chance. Then again, do you think he would have succeeded in his first attempt? It took him two more years to get a little recognition. In total, it's a ten-year struggle that helped him become this big a name."

"But Lala ji, a small meeting with him is all we ask for, please. I humbly request you."

"No possibility, my kids. Otherwise, you wouldn't have had to request twice."

How smart Upasna's father has played with me. A politician in every sense of the word. Giving me something unrealistic would have exposed him. Therefore, he chose to play smart. Gave me something that sounded realistic, yet far from reality. He wanted to check my courage and stuff, my foot. I felt weak, helpless and terrible. Everything requires time, I thought in my mind; every single thing. In a period of 15 months, no one can lay a foundation so strong and here I am, expected to start off with my plan for a lifetime.

We got up thanking that teddy bear for his time. I was feeling a huge sense of disappointment within myself. We had come seeking help with a strong sense of hope. Instead, all we got was advice. I was cursing myself for raising the level of expectation from this meeting. I reminded myself that life is not easy and people aren't meant to help.

My impatience was triggering the eagerness inside me. I wanted to get up and act. Nonetheless, I had no idea to act upon. I wanted to start off right away, maximum in a day or two, or at that moment itself. I did not want to waste any time, and instead wanted to conquer the world. I had limited time, and none to squander. The pressure was getting the better of me.

I was frustrated enough to not realize I was sitting in the car after having reached my place for almost half an hour. I connected my phone with the audio player and played my favourite song 'You are beautiful' by James Blunt. I could never decipher what was in that song that made me love it so much. Were it the lyrics that beautifully described the helplessness of a lover or the voice modulation. Whatever it was, there was something magical about it for me, always. Next, I played 'Bonfire Heart' by the same singer. My second favourite to connect me to peace.

Upasna's video call interrupted it in the very beginning. I cut the call, but she called again. I cut it again. She called again. I picked it up this time. It took a while for the internet to connect us face to face. She was in her room in her usual office formals, indicating she had just reached after finishing work. She had a white pillow in her lap.

"Why was my call not being taken?" she asked, very sternly.

"I was trying to keep problems away," I jokingly said.

She smiled at my sentence, a wide sparkling smile. Her eyes twinkled with grace.

"I am sorry to disappoint you, but I am not leaving, sir. Not even a break up can work," she retorted.

"That's like my sweet girl," I said

"How have you been, my love?" she then asked

"How can a failed man be?" I acted, seeking sympathy.

"Since when have you started talking like that? Everything alright?" She was concerned.

"I don't think I am worthy of being with you, Upasna. It was my first day of the challenge, and it feels like I am already broken," I expressed.

"You don't have to think this way, Paarth," she said. "Give your best and leave the rest."

"So you mean, umm.... Should I leave you?"

"Should I break you?"

I laughed.

"All of this that you have done, from giving up American PR to taking up a job in Chandigarh, how can it be so easy on you?" I asked.

"We all sacrifice for people we love. All of us. I am not the first person. Nor the last," she replied politely.

"I consider myself lucky. I wish I can make you feel the same," I said.

"I already feel lucky, Paarth. I already do," she said.

"But I have done nothing for you. Not a single thing ever. I haven't even bought you a twenty-rupee chocolate till date. Never even cared to assure you of stability and a safe future through words."

"You have done what was essential for our relationship to grow, just know that."

"Can I ask you what I have done that you feel is enough?" I asked.

"You value the efforts I make for you. Seldom do you fail to acknowledge them," was her simple answer.

"Is that enough? I don't think so. That's not even the basic."

"Trust me, it's more than one can ask for. I mean, the biggest cause of couples breaking up or relationships not working is this. People fail to respect efforts made for them. They do that sometimes out of ego, or sometimes out of taking someone for granted. The other person isn't a fool, you see. You've got to be kind enough to appreciate someone's gestures towards you."

"Well, well, well… Your words redeem all the bad stuff I dealt with today," I said.

"Come into my arms," she said lovingly. "Let me heal you."

"I really wish I could," I said, craving to feel her.

"Close your eyes. Imagine walking up to me," she said softly.

"Ahan!" I muttered, quite under her spell.

"I stand in silence, looking at you, wearing my heart on my sleeves. There is a wish in my eyes. There are flames rising in them. With every step that you take towards me, it makes my heart beat faster. It makes me feel you are reading my mind. You know I want to melt."

I look at her image on my phone screen, dazed. Like I could just extend my hand and hold her.

"You come close, you take my hands in yours, and put your lips on my forehead. I feel every inch of them, closing my eyes. I move my head, craving to feel your kisses everywhere. On my nose. My cheeks. My lips. My chin."

I cannot hold back anymore. "Then I take your face in my hands. Kiss you softly on the nose, and slowly moving downwards, draw your lips towards mine, to lock them with mine, holding you tight in my arms."

"That is intense," she says and breaks into a smile.

"I still don't believe that destiny brought me to you."

"Sometimes I am scared about how much I love you. How much I want to be with you. How much I wish to make you happy," she said most adorably.

"You are the cause for all my happiness, Upasna."

"I don't have any reason why I do what I do for you. All I know is, you are my sweetest mission, Paarth. I am pursuing you with all my heart. I am not even sure if this will last forever, for we have no control over fate, but I can tell you very prudently, every moment that I have spent with you, talking or thinking, I have felt complete."

"Keep going," her words were like a soothing balm on my burning heart.

"Excuse me? You are the writer here, it's you who must express it. Now start! I want to listen."

I took a deep breath, smiling. "Okay," I said. "When you say my name, it feels like I am worthy of all the good things in life. I feel as if the best season of the year is around. The best time to live is here. I feel everything is good. Like everything that is happening was meant to happen, and add to my happiness."

"Wow, poetic. Don't you stop!"

I smiled and started over. "Even I am surprised why I put your happiness before mine. I don't understand how that is possible with any human being. Or if that is what we call true love. It's important for me... more than breathing, to know that you are safe. Trust me, I don't want to love you like that. It takes away the peace of my mind. But the fact of the matter is, every inch of me is all about caring for you. I feel you are the only reason I try to grow. If I have to explain myself in one word, I'll say, 'irritating'. I can very easily lose my temper on things that I don't like, and I would want them to change almost immediately. But with you, it's the other way round. I am in love with your faults. I am in love with your scars. I am in love with your imperfections. I don't want you to change. There is a feeling that binds us together, and fits me into this world. No matter for how long I keep going on and on, the truth is, I'll never be able to express what you mean to me. I still remember, once you told me all about the importance of having a good relationship with parents. You even showed me the way. Today, I often ask god why we met so late. My life would have been so much better and easier with you there. You bring out the best I can be. Thank you for each and every single minute of being mine."

We had tears rolling down our eyes as I spoke. The words had just brought forth the purest form of love we felt for each other.

"Come closer to the camera," she said. "Bring your forehead closer."

She leaned forward and kissed.

"I love you so much," she said.

"I love you," I said.

That was the confidence I needed to see in that weak moment, maybe. So with more responsibility and seriousness, I began to plan things up. Upasna's love was a huge motivation. Since her support was by my side, I could easily take this fight to the very last point.

Obviously, I had no idea where to start from, but when you walk in the dark with all faith in god and have good intentions, things start working your way. That's an undefeated rule of nature. People often fail to understand as to when exactly the universe conspires to grant them the wishes that they want with all their heart. Well, in this very rule lies the answer.

Lost in a world of my own, I was surfing through a few television channels when my phone rang. I took the call and spoke to the caller for a while. Some work related issue. After the end of that brief conversation, I saw an interview being aired on the television channel. I raised the volume to hear Balwant Khosla talking. The most renowned Pollywood producer was sharing views on his upcoming projects and was announcing signing Gurdas Mann for his next film. He was standing outside a residential building and talking. The backdrop read, Eden Apartments, Sector 88, Mohali.

"Does he live here?" I asked myself. "Is it a signal god is giving me to start off from?"

I approached the one person who could answer me correctly. The security personnel of that society.

"Which producer are you looking for?" he asked as I stood at the entrance.

"Which? What do you mean by which?" I said.

"Many of them live here. Whom are you looking for?"

Before I could answer, he asked me to walk a few steps back as he opened the gate to an Audi A6.

"Now this was Surjeet Bansal, the director of *Guddiyan* movie. He also lives here." The security guy said. "Whom do you want to meet?"

"Can you give me a list of all the Pollywood big shots who live here? Only the producers and the directors?" I requested.

"How would I have a list?" he said. "Moreover, I am not allowed to share anyone's details with you. That is strictly against the policy. I could lose my job if someone got a whiff of this."

I thought for a while. He was morally and professionally right. At the cost of his job, he wasn't going to do anything for a person who was asking questions that were more suspicious than general. My million pleas would not have convinced him either. Hence, I decided to be brutally truthful. I decided to narrate my story to him. If he could sense purity, he would help me; if not, then I would accept it as my fate.

The security person was an emotional Punjabi. A kind man who would listen to you and sensitively feel every word that you say. It melted his heart to learn the efforts I was making for a girl. He appreciated the fact that I was sincere for someone when all he saw were people bringing in different girls every day to their flats and using them for sexual pleasure. Appreciating me to have told him everything with honesty, he wrote the names of whatever producers and directors lived there. Fortunately for me, he knew the office addresses of some of them too, and he wrote them down for me. He went a step ahead by mentioning the names of other residential areas where some of them put up.

Slowly, in a few days' time, I figured out that most directors and producers were based in New Mohali or outer Mohali region. I also figured out on observation that they often went to gyms and regularly visited bars in Chandigarh for their meetings. It was roughly twenty kilometres from where I lived. I decided to spend at least three evenings in a week chasing these people.

Like for my manuscript, the publishers would turn me down, I knew I was going to see the same fate for the screenplay as well. Therefore, I prepared myself mentally to take failures and still find resilience till I succeeded.

One thing I had accepted and learnt at that age was that every failure was a stepping stone, if you had the larger picture in your mind. Life gives you opportunities at different stages. The thing to know is, they won't come shouting out to you. They will come wearing the mask of a problem that you want to run away from. People who find enough courage to stand still and face it are able to unmask and know the real chance behind it. The rest, however, run away and regret later. Upasna's coming into my life, I presumed, was for this particular reason. For my career growth, which I would have never pushed for otherwise.

I started off with visiting their offices. The first person I went to hunt for was the most renowned producer of the industry – Balwant Khosla. They made me sit outside his office for around eight hours. Then, they came out and said that Mr Khosla had to leave for some urgent work.

"Is it a bloody joke going on here?" I shouted at him in my head. I felt disappointed that I wasn't even given a chance. Moreover, I lost on my taxi business as well for one entire day. But anyhow, this beginning was absolutely in sync with my expectations from it. I asked them before leaving if I could come back the next day. Their precise reply was, "If you wish to."

I wondered if I was the only party interested. As if this producer doesn't need a good story to film. I retorted with a smile that I would.

Next day was an add-on to the previous day. Sat there for around eight hours again, with no result. The third day was the same. Fourth day. Same. Fifth day. Same. Sixth day. Same. This went on for not a few days or weeks, but for a good two months. Neither was I disappointed, nor was I not disappointed. It was pretty obvious that one doesn't get such a break so soon. However, if I missed the timeline, any success would have no meaning.

Kartik jumped in to help, understanding the need of the hour. By hearing the stories I had written and running around to cover the maximum number of producers that he personally could. Discussing our experiences of rejections was the most memorable thing of those times. It usually started in a depressed state, cursing life and abusing the arrogance of producers and directors, but ended up making both of us laugh, readying us for the hindrances of the next day.

I need to confess here, that he tried to reach out to these people with the same spirit and aggression I was exuberating. If I was giving up on my sleep to make things work, he was doing the same, without me having to ask for it. It was a separate topic altogether that he would bump into a girl in these offices each day, or while following them, and would each time be handed a blunt rejection. But then, he knew, this was his only chance to get a girlfriend. Because shaadi.com, just like Tinder, didn't change much for him.

I began to drink those days. Nothing was in excess, but the frequency had increased quite a bit. After an entire day of driving or sitting in the car in anticipation of passengers, then hunting for a time slot for making my story be heard was taking a toll on my body. I had the least amount of sleep, because I had so much to worry about. My stress levels were so high that even when my eyes were closed, my mind was working aggressively to find a way out.

My conversations with Upasna were now confined to just about fifteen to twenty minutes every day. Both of us took a mature decision for our future. Not only in ours, but in every relationship, people must understand that when they are building themselves, they must let their love life wait. It's like a long term investment. By giving less time in the present moment, you are basically making a ground to be together forever. I was stressed. I could see some grey hair popping up on my head.

One fine night, I sat on the stairs of a bar, waiting for a producer to finish with his dinner. He had promised to listen to me and given me a time of ten minutes to describe my story. I had rehearsed it for a thousand times. Despite practicing it, I was nervous. I knew I could not afford to fumble or stop, so that I could convey every idea quickly. Secondly, I was shivering. It was 4 degrees Celsius and the visibility due to fog had reduced down to just a few metres. My clothes were not enough, it seemed, and the cold had started getting to me. It was the first time I was actually going to speak before a producer, after toiling for about six months.

After every few seconds, I would turn back to check if he had come out. It made me feel like a beggar at the mercy of someone else. I recollected myself and told confidently that this time would pass before I know and I would make sure I never feel the same again.

I ran after the producer as he came out of the bar, storming towards his car.

"Sir, sir…" I ran towards him, seeking his attention. What if he thought I had gone off! I had to be prompt.

"You have 600 seconds to go," he said, putting a cigarette in his mouth.

I came to the point straight away. Very enthusiastically and animatedly, I began to narrate the story to him. I picked the momentum from a certain point and took it higher through my pitch and tone. The director didn't look at me even once. He was all in his cigarette, relishing the escape it gave. It popped a question in my mind, if he was doing a mere formality of listening to me? I continued nevertheless. My spirit didn't come down an ounce. I held my energy high.

We had been walking the talk, and had now reached his car. He stood there for only until he was done with his cigarette. The moment it was done; he didn't give me a second to go on. He jumped inside his car and drove away. I followed the car, talking into his window, as if possessed. The car vanished within a few seconds. I stood there, watching in disbelief what had just happened. Just then, a Fortuner hit me from behind. I flew a few feet above the ground before getting my forehead banged.

I didn't breathe for a few seconds. I realized something was dripping from my forehead, most likely blood. I was feeling a severe irritation on my knees and palms. I rubbed my hands on my trousers and checked myself for any major injuries, if any.

Tears rolled down my eyes. I was being squashed through humiliation. At the end of every day, it was difficult to look at myself in the eyes. My self-esteem was continuously being hurt.

At the next opportunity I got, I was beaten up mercilessly by a couple of bouncers. The director was walking with the cast of a movie. They had reached Elante Mall for its promotion. I jumped over the barricades to convince him to listen. Behind me, many youngsters followed. The bouncers jumped in before them, considering me to be an intruder too. A punch landed on my face. It felt as if someone had hit me with a rock. I spun like a tornado and boom! Another punch. This time on my head. My nose began to bleed profusely. My head went numb.

I had been feeling let down and humiliated in many ways, thanks to the varied experiences in the past few months. Then I went digital too. I signed up for an account on Facebook and Twitter. I made sure I had sent synopsis of my story to each and every director I could find.

Whenever they would post a picture or anything, I used to be among the first ones to comment, so that it caught their eyes. I would even drop my number, requesting them to contact in case they were interested. Random people called me, playing pranks of being the director. Towards the end, they would laugh out loud making fun of me. Though I did not see the joke in these prank calls.

My struggle in those days took a toll on my relationship with Upasna. I wasn't talking to her with the same warmth I earlier used to. It wasn't that I was mad at her for she was the reason I was in this situation. It was the reflection of my own worth that I wasn't able to handle. I had begun to shout at her for every small thing. She was taking all my frustration quietly. She knew where this odd side of me was coming from.

Even after all the bad things I said to her, she never protested. Every single time this happened, she maintained faith in the power of devotion. I was sure she would regret many things in solitude because that's when your heart plays havoc on your thoughts. Just that she didn't have the habit of mentioning her troubles to anyone. She always was mature. Always the one who loved me more.

Later on, when I was quickly running out of time, I slipped handouts of the detailed synopsis of my story through the doors of these directors' houses. On the last page, I would mention my contact details. No response ever came. Like a weirdo or lunatic, I would expect every unknown caller to be someone interested in filming my story. But unlike in films, no magic happened for me. Nothing ever changed. I had run out of all my ideas of selling the story.

It was the last day of the fifteen months given to me. I was invited to Upasna's house again. She was wearing a dark green suit with golden danglers in her ears that played hide and seek. There were waves in her hair. She hadn't used any make up on her face, and yet, she looked beautiful. It was simplicity at its mesmerizing best.

I sat in the same place in the drawing room where I had first met her father all those months back. This time, though, the difficulty level had been raised. It was not only him, but also Upasna's mother who was sitting in front of me as a judge. Upasna nervously stood beside the single sofa that I had occupied. She was well aware of the status of my situation. It was out of hands now.

"You have gained, my son. Especially on the cheeks. Beer effect?" Upasna's father commented.

I laughed. "No, sir. That happens with age, I guess."

"For that matter, why don't you look at Upasna's mother!" He laughed, winking at her. "She is still as fit and fabulous as when I first met her."

"Don't embarrass me, Ram. Come on!" she said, her cheeks turning pink.

I pretended I was intrigued. I looked at Upasna from the corner of my eyes. She was rubbing her hands, checking me out.

"Why don't you grab a cup of coffee? Upasna..." Upasna's father said.

'I am okay, sir," I interrupted. "It's fine." I signalled to Upasna, who had almost taken a step towards the kitchen.

Any liquid in a stressful situation can lead to frequent urination. I applauded myself for the correct decision.

Upasna's father picked up a newspaper that lay on the table. He carefully read something on the front page for a minute, only to be stopped by his wife's elbow. He wrapped it up quickly, apologizing.

"I am sorry! Newspapers are my weakness, you see. It takes over me as soon as I see it," he said.

"No issues, sir," I said.

"What's your take on the presently formed government, Paarth? Do you think any good thing is happening to our nation?" Upasna's father asked.

"I don't take interest in politics, sir. Not my cup of tea."

"But why? If we aren't aware, how will we play our part in the change?"

"Maybe by doing with honesty whatever we choose to do," I said.

"Interesting," he said. "Honesty is an important thing for sure."

A tiny break of a few seconds followed. Nobody spoke anything. After the ice breakers, it was finally time to take the topic in hand.

"We had a conversation a few months back," he continued normally, rubbing his neatly trimmed beard. "In context of it, I hope you won't mind answering everything as fairly as possible."

"Absolutely, sir," I said.

"We would love if you can explain what have you been able to manifest all this while? What plans you have made? Why did you formulate…and all that stuff?

I took a deep breath, and ignoring their questions, I began illustrating in detail my crammed part on how things kick-started for me. I had prepared good enough content just the day before, after immense deliberation. It was like a modest self-appreciation letter that accounted my inspiring journey through troubles.

I highlighted my limitations to them, which weren't one or two in terms of my awareness and resources, but plenty. The very realization that I did not have much to choose from hurt my courage. Because you always need certain alternatives to go for the best. Nevertheless, I said, I accepted my situation without grumbling, and I had to do what I had to do. It was pretty much a challenge to control my desperation and keep myself patient as I was getting carried away and feeling I was under the hammer. There were a thousand vague ideas that occurred in my head almost every second. Most of them were senseless and non-feasible.

"Cut it, cut it, cut it!" Upasna's father stopped me. "Just explain to me what you did, are doing and plan to do for a stable living."

"Ok, sir," I said reframing everything, and demonstrated how I decided to sell my story to directors and producers, and the manner in which I went about with it, the low moments I experienced and how I managed rejections.

"Do you think this can give you lifelong income and a smooth life?" her mother asked. "This is pretty much dependent upon luck, don't you think? It's a very unpredictable and dark road."

"Of course, ma'am. There is a huge risk in what I am doing. But writers earn well in modern times. Plus, it is a very prestigious career path, I feel," I said.

"Writing stories for movies? Will only that help? Because you are aiming for Punjabi cinema in particular. I don't think they pay that well," her mom said.

"Ma'am, Upasna must have told you that I write books too," I said.

"But only one has been published till date na? Less than a thousand copies sold and rest being rejected, isn't it?"

"Yes, ma'am. I am sorry," I said, embarrassed.

Where is the conversation headed? I thought to myself. I was told they only want to see my effort and nothing else. This is clear cheating.

"So, what was the ultimate result? Were you able to sell your story to some production house?" her father jumped in with his next direct question.

It blew off the color from Upasna's face. The ultimate question that would have decided our future was here. I looked at Upasna and smiled.

Then, I stood up and picked up my small carry bag from the floor. I took out ten bundles of thousand rupee notes from it. Very modestly, I kept the money on the table. It was ten lakh rupees in total.

"I have been able to sell the film rights for the two stories I wrote. The publishers rejected them, but someone found them good enough to be filmed. Shri Devi Dyal Productions have decided to take them up for filming, and the shooting shall begin in three months after the cast is finalized."

"Oh my god!" exclaimed Upasna in joy. She was unaware till the last moment. I had decided to keep it a secret, to surprise her and to see the look of happiness on her face. Her parents were fascinated by my accomplishment. They had their mouths open.

"But I have to mention something very important," I added seriously, getting slower in tone and louder with my pitch, "Before we celebrate this, please take note that my name won't be displayed in the story credits anywhere."

"What?" Her father said in shock. "What are you talking about?"

"Sir, I won't be given the credit of writing these stories; someone else would be."

"Someone else would be.... and not you?" He muttered, unable to digest what I had said.

He continued, "Who on earth sells their stories, leaving credits behind? Do you even understand the value a writer's name holds for him? It's his name that fetches him income throughout his life. And you compromised with that?"

"Sir, I took the opportunity that I got, and I loved Upasna, so I thought I should take this road. This was the only chance I could create for myself."

"You can't love someone by letting your brain remain jammed," Upasna's mother said.

"By bringing in these ten lakh rupees, which you might be thinking is an astonishing achievement, you have actually let a life-changing opportunity go, Paarth," her father continued.

"Papa, please..." Upasna interrupted.

"In the first place, I don't understanding how writing or selling stories can earn you a good living. Secondly, after what Paarth has done, even if I help him to establish a business, I am sure he will squander it. His exposure is very limited, and I can't risk my daughter with him."

"You are being very unfair, Papa," Upasna revolted.

"Unfair? Just for I love you Upasna, I agreed to give him a chance. I didn't care what society would say about me. I didn't let my attention divert to how people would humiliate me on letting you marry him. On social status, he isn't close. His education, unfortunately, is not up to the mark. He is four years younger to you. Still I don't want to judge him on his background and I respect him for who he is, however you both must understand that you are no match."

"Papa, we have managed to be with each other through this time. We certainly have a great understanding," Upasna tried to explain.

"Both of you are kids. Life is tough and complicated. You two should walk your ways and look for a suitable partner," her father said with a sort of finality.

"Papa.... but...."

"No Upasna. If Paarth really loves you, he can prove it by respectfully leaving. You deserve certain things that he can't afford. He should empathize, know his current status, and take a decision that we all want to accept."

I looked at Upasna. She had tried her best. I grabbed my money from the table, stood up and I left, thanking everyone for their time.

A few minutes later, I received a text from Upasna,

I am extremely sorry for my parents' behaviour. They said things they shouldn't have. Even I was surprised at how my father treated you. I have never seen this side of him before. I wish I could go back in time and stop him. Please forgive me for today.

I didn't reply to the message. I read and logged off from my phone.

At midnight, Upasna texted again,

Kindly check your email. I have sent something very important! Read every word very carefully.

I opened my mail box and clicked on her email. It read:

Dear Paarth,

I wish I could close my eyes and when I opened them back, this would be a nightmare. Alas! What I feared the most has come before me. I never thought it would ever reach this point of separation, and it's ridiculous that I am the one responsible for it. I have acted with immaturity and I know my family and I have hurt you.

Know that you are the most wonderful person I have ever come across. With or without anything, I wanted to live with you. You often say you have never done anything for me. This old habit of yours of never counting what you give is too adorable. People often do a little for others and repeatedly speak a lot about it. I found someone in you who offered help to the world and forgot about it. Could never decide if you are just naturally this nice, or you were like this for just me.

I want to thank you for something really kind. In all our years of being together, only talking to me mattered to you. Every time we met, your only intention was to spend time with me. You spoke what you had in your heart, and always listened to what I wanted to say attentively. You never asked for sex, or for any sort of physical intimacy when you knew I wouldn't have said no to you.

In all these years, we had some extraordinary conversations that give me goosebumps even now. I am sure you feel the same whenever you recall them.

On days when I sit to think what true love is, I realize it's not rocket science, or how complicated the world portrays it to be. Give your best. Care like a mother. Never ask or expect in return. This is how simple it actually is. I am honored to have walked the path of it holding your hand. I can very proudly go out and acknowledge before the world that true love exists and I have lived that.

You are a personification of innocence. What you feel in your heart, you convey in your words. I hope you continue to be the same for the rest of your life. I have stored each and every single screenshot of all our conversations till date.

That being said, I am sorry to say that I'll have to take the path my parents choose for me. I tried my best to convince them, but maybe I am not lucky enough to live my dreams.

I can surely leave their side and come to you. That is indeed one easy option. But the point is, if I fail to show loyalty towards them today, I'll never be able to show loyalty for you. Like always, I hope you understand me today as well. If not, please don't hate me. I am helpless, and I do look like a loser today.

Life is going to be tough from here, but I'll love you till the end of time.

The one in whose heart you will live forever,

Upasna

I surprisingly gave a very strange reaction to her letter, and that was – no reaction. I didn't feel angry. I didn't show signs of regret. Neither was I sad. Nor did I take it as the end of the world. Maybe my conscious was aware that missing out on me for Upasna wasn't a huge loss practically. Or maybe my love for Upasna was so much that I always evaluated a situation in terms of her gain all the time. The worst option her parents could avail as husband for her would have been a million times ahead of me, I thought.

On the financial front, social front, career front, security front – I was lacking in every sense. Therefore, keeping that in mind and accepting that whatever happened was for Upasna's better, I tried to get as less emotional as possible and wrote a very toned down reply to her email.

Dear Upasna,

I thought of not replying to you at first. I mean, what's the point in dragging a topic when there is seemingly no future together for the people involved? But then, that wouldn't have been right on my part, because it's not your fault, any of this. You earnestly tried your best in this whole relationship, and despite all efforts you made, I failed you. I failed this bond.

I am sorry for whatever I could have done right, and did not. Coming to your decision of accepting your parents' wish, I respect what you have decided to go with. I get it, it's tough to be an Indian girl sometimes. When torn between parents and lover, it's most of the times right to choose the former over the latter. You aren't doing anything wrong, because one, this is not in your hands, and second, there is no sense in taking the most important step of one's life without the blessings of people who have raised us.

You have already done enough for me. I would never want you to take another step that can eventually disappoint many people who have their hopes tied to you, who you don't want to hurt in any way. I am obliged and overwhelmed by as much time you were able to give.

I will never be able to forget the day I saw you for the first time. I wish I could put that feeling into words; but nothing can explain what I felt at that moment. When you told me you loved me, it was a once in a lifetime moment for me. I literally lived a fantasy that night. For me, to be so loved by a girl like you, I don't think I even had the audacity to have it in my wildest dream.

In you, for the first time I met someone who thought like me. You were like my own reflection. I knew if there is something I can't say, you will still know what I would have said. Precisely. My soul is connected with you. So, thank you for everything.

As far as this situation goes, let's be real and practical. Life won't stop, and neither would it turn out bad. Just that it won't be as good as it could have been with both of us together.

Much love and regards,
Paarth

Years of a beautiful relationship ended in just a moment. I had made our relationship my roots, and I felt I was handicapped now. It was like someone held my hand, put me into a time machine and dropped me to the lowest point from my past. All my dedication and sincerity went to waste, it seemed. Six years full of love and hope, spent painting a future together, and here came the moment of realization that the next sixty she won't be there for me to even see. I felt a severe pain in my chest, imagining she would grow old with someone else, and I... I'll just be a forgotten thing from the past.

Maybe I was a loser at everything. I don't deny; I was incapable, imbecile and brainless as well. But I always gave my best for her. For she was my number one, my favourite place, thing, friend and partner. I cared for her like no one else ever could. Unfortunately, I could not wish the same from someone else for her because I knew that was just not possible. Two souls feeling an age-old connection doesn't happen every day. It happens just once in life, and I was losing that chance in front of my eyes.

She loved me even on days when I would regret being me. With her, failure could never give me pain, misfortune could never take my hope away, defeat could never lessen my effort, and pain could never take my smile away. Bad times did come, yes, they certainly did once in a while, but together, we could beat it and come out victorious.

The next morning was the first in six years when I didn't receive a good morning message from her. Nobody asked me if I had had my breakfast. Neither did I feel responsible enough to have it. I knew she wasn't waiting on the other side for me to finish with mine or else she was going to wait for hers. It was funny how things can change so quickly. Someone who is so important to you vanishes all of a sudden. Gone, to never return. You don't have a right on them anymore, and they have no place for you. It's strange!

Maybe that's what is known as complexity of a situation, which can bring about any consequence. I picked up all the writing pads, pens from my room and locked them in my room. I wasn't going to write for a while now. Professionally, maybe, I wasn't going to try writing again. What had it got me!

People say nothing lasts forever. But, let's ponder honestly – do we cease to feel the love of someone when they are gone from the world? Absolutely not! Their feelings, their memories remain. Always. So does their love.

In the afternoon, when I was collecting money from a passenger whom I had dropped at Elante Mall, my phone beeped. After giving them the change, I checked my phone. I had received an email from a literary agent. After Upasna told me she had written emails to me and I hadn't seen, I had become more attentive to it. But what use was it now! I still read the email.

Dear Mr Paarth,

I am pleased to inform you that after a meticulous examination of your script, we have decided to represent you. We have attached an agreement which you can go through. In case you are satisfied with all the conditions, please send us signed copies in duplicate.

We will pitch your manuscript to various leading publishers in the country and get back to you within a week with a positive reply, hopefully.

Regards,
Amrit Sehgal

I opened the trail mail to check my initiation email to them. I had sent it a year before and now was when I got an answer to it. Even snails moved faster than these people in the literary industry, I muttered.

I read the agent's email again. What happiness I received reading those words of acceptance! Half a decade I had waited for it. Half a damn decade! My patience at last had been rewarded. Was this the opening that I wanted as a novelist? Was this the news that would turn everything around?

"Surely, yes!" My heart exclaimed. I was on cloud nine and all smiles.

Ecstatic as I was supposed to be, I typed a text to Upasna before it occurred to me that we were no longer together. My happiness suddenly vanished, realizing that things were no longer the same. I looked at the typed message, confused. For a few seconds I thought I should press the send button. Then I thought I must avoid texting her. Yes/No, Yes/No – I was in a big doubt.

I pressed my lips tight, closed my fist and erased off the message in the end. I looked in the distance, feeling lost. I gave one final thought to it. Should I inform her or would it be better left untold? I threw the phone away, half smiling at my luck. When I had desperately waited for this, no positive answer from anyone came up. Now, when this least mattered or I had no one to share the news with, I was getting a break.

I thought I won't reply to the agent unless he sent me a reminder. At least I could be sure he really wanted to represent it. I was still lost in thought, if not informing Upasna was the right decision. I earnestly wanted to feel the joy and happiness in her words, because her desperation of seeing me do well was similar to mine. If I had waited every second of the last six years for a chance to become a writer, to see my book in print, she too had asked for that for me in every prayer she made. Nevertheless, for me, what came out more important as per my understanding was that unlike before, when I crazily used to wait for these people to revert, I had grown into the complete opposite. Not that I had lost interest, no! I was just sad that Upasna wasn't there to share the joy.

The unthinkable did happen, though. The agent reached out to me again, and was taking things forward on my behalf after the agreement was signed. Quite unlike my earlier self, I did not work on any follow up this time. And look how strange destiny's ways are! Within three days of receiving the copy of the agreement signed by me, he fetched me a deal from one of the best publishing houses of the country.

I was sent an advance of eighty thousand rupees, and the book was supposed to be released in a year. The contract I received from the publisher was the biggest accomplishment of my life. I cried like a child, holding it close to my chest. Its weight was worth in gold. However, Upasna's and my father's absence played a huge spoilsport in the celebrations.

So I met my partner in all crimes, Kartik, to talk my heart out. He would never leave my side, I knew. Even when he knew I was wrong or at fault, he would stay by me, because he knew too well I would have a reason. Even if that made him suffer along with me, he would stay. In his company, I felt relieved and less burdened. Both of us sat on the small mound of gravel next to a tea stall on the outer Zirakpur region. It was mainly on the side of the highway road. Behind us was a wall on which a middle-aged man was painting slogans in Hindi. We had just finished with tea and held the empty glasses in our hands and had been talking about random stuff.

"Did you tell aunty about it? What was her reaction? I am sure she must have been proud?" Kartik asked, very enthusiastically.

I smiled at his excitement. His expectation was far from the reality. "She was happy to see me happy, and the fact that our bank balance inflated. But otherwise, she doesn't understand the importance of writing and all that. She isn't, you know, much educated. She only understands government jobs. Safety, security, regular income," I said nodding my head.

"She knows it well; you aren't eligible for entrance exams. You never went to college," Kartik said.

"You can't explain things to people who live with strong perceptions. Better ignore them and save your time and energy," I said matter of factly, like I didn't care.

"Why do you have to talk like this?" Kartik said, a little taken aback. "Sometimes you empathize so well, and sometimes, you are just another person."

"She told me books gave me one lakh rupees after nothing less than five or six years. She thinks I should give it up and focus on driving and film writing," I said.

"That's fine." He said, laughing, "So she calculated your monthly income in her mind! Roughly sits to Rs 1600 a month."

"Yeah," I muttered, throwing a stone in the distance.

Kartik's voice mellowed suddenly. "I am surprised though," Kartik said. "You did what you used to say you would do. I remember how in school, other students would gather and make fun of your claims."

"What about you? Did you also do that with them, huh?" I asked.

"I never spoke anything, I swear. I only enjoyed what they used to say about you," Kartik said. "After all, you are my breast friend." He winked at me and said, "I crack jokes on you in person only."

"So you won't be making fun of me today?" I said.

"Just not for a few hours. I'll be back to normal soon enough," Kartik said.

I looked at him smiling. "So you do know when I am down and you must avoid being stupid?"

"How much money in your bank account now? A million?" Kartik guessed, ignoring my question.

I nodded. "Highest bank balance ever."

"Where are you going to spend all of it? Saving it, or buying something for yourself?"

"Na! Need to get the house renovated," I said.

"Argghh, that's terrible. It will be gone then. That would leave you nothing to enjoy with."

"Yeah man! That's like bad luck. You can only enjoy when your father leaves behind enough money. Otherwise, whatever you earn, you have to use it for family."

"Seems like we are born to be servants," Kartik said. "First twenty years, live the way parents want; the rest of your life in service of a girl and your notorious kids."

"You think you have grown old enough?" A voice interrupted us. "Didn't read the manual of life before coming into this world?"

The painter had been curiously listening to us. We turned back to his words, and he walked close to us and stood, his hands in his pocket.

He pierced into my eyes when he said, "Don't ponder over what you can derive from your actions. Move on and focus on what you must do, my friend! Here you are regretting not inheriting wealth, something you think you must have been entitled to. But you are wrong! You must earn for yourself, and see having no resources as the best opportunity."

"Sorry?" I said.

"If you had everything already, and you had just compounded it, it would have been no big deal. With sensibility, anyone can do it. I can do it too. However, when you have nothing and you create things, the world stands up to salute your courage," the painter said.

We did not react. Both of us were expressionless. We mainly behaved like two arrogant youngsters who were merely hearing him out to get rid of him sooner.

"If you nurture such negativity in your head, dear friends, you will never be able to enjoy life," he said with a smile.

"Sleep over this! Despite the fact that you have reached the highest bank balance in your life, ever, you are not happy. A million rupees is not a small amount, and you are not happy owning it. You are sad that you won't be able to spend it on your selfish and wasteful motives. How silly of you!"

Kartik and I looked at each other, thinking.

"Life has given you an opportunity to enjoy. You think you will have the same thing happening again? Maybe no. Maybe yes. It's uncertain. What life brings tomorrow, only god knows. So why don't you cheer up today and choose to look at the brighter side of things? Can you answer me? Can you answer yourself?"

I wondered wherefrom such negativity had trickled into my blood? Why did I not think the way this painter had? So simply, and so wisely! I am supposed to be a writer. What hope will I convey to people if I am myself so immature in my actions. It was like waking up to reality.

"What if this had never happened and you were living the same dull life? You would, in that case, have been praying to reach this stage. Today, when you actually have this, when this has been given to you on your request or hard work or whatever, you are searching for yet another reason to be disappointed. Tell me one thing, boys! Are you born idiots or natural pessimists?" he said.

"Consider yourself lucky," he looked at me and said. "You have a chance to take the growth of your family forward.

It's not called waste of money. It's not called a situation of misery. It is not missing out on anything."

"You are right, sir," I muttered, my glare fixed on him. "I realize it."

"Life isn't about dancing to loud music in exclusive bars. It has been wrongly marketed to your generation, I am sure. You have fallen to the conspiracy of an industry that wants to earn money by making you believe their rubbish ideas of a good life. You are only enjoying when you are living to the fullest. Afraid of no challenges, carried away by no joy. You are the master of what you feel. Because you only feel what you make yourself feel!"

"I can sense wisdom in your words. Thank you so much, sir," Kartik said.

"No need to mention that, young man." The painter said, "Just take care of what I said, if it made sense to you."

Both of us very obediently nodded our heads.

"Would you like to have tea with us?" I asked.

"It's my work time. Maybe some other day, if we meet," he replied and walked off towards his tin of paint.

"You paint extremely well, and look at your handwriting...," I said.

"Thank you!" he said, smiling, waving it away humbly.

"You learnt it in school... or from somewhere else?" Kartik asked.

"I have never gone to school," he said without any regret in his voice.

"How can you do this then?" I asked, curious. "I think this requires education. At least the spellings."

"My father was a painter. He taught me everything," he retorted.

"Wow, that is even more impressive," I said.

He smiled and then added lightly, "I am glad I don't belong to the category of painters who write 'child bear' instead of 'chilled beer'." We all laughed.

"By the way, do you guys know what the score is? It's India–Pakistan cricket match today," he asked.

"I can tell you the rate. Interested for a bet?" Kartik said in the same light spirit.

"I don't think I'll want to risk my children's school fee."

"They go to school?" I asked.

"Of course! They must do what I wasn't able to. I don't want them to depend on odd jobs."

"You aren't happy with this?" I asked.

"What is happiness, my friend? I am more than satisfied with what I have. I thank god I am able to feed my family, and live with no regrets. I am able to get a sound sleep every night, and my needs are bare minimum."

"What a man!" I whispered, impressed. "I am going to write this conversation in my book. He is very inspiring."

"But don't you want to have a car, a big house and a better life? Maybe not for comfort... but for raising the quality of your life."

"I have faith, when I am prepared to handle them, I'll have them."

"And what if you don't have them ever?"

"I'll know I was never prepared to handle them."

"Don't you think it's more like fooling oneself?" I wanted to know what he was thinking. This was a strange way of looking at life.

"If it keeps my heart and mind clean, and I don't have to live craving when I know my pocket won't allow, it's okay to live like a fool," he said with a smile.

"I am not convinced with it," I shook my head.

"Change the way you have always thought. Experiment a bit with the way your brain is programmed. You will understand what I am advocating."

I went forward and hugged him for his brilliant piece of life lesson, and jumped on Kartik's bike. The painter had a gifted smile and was a healer in the true sense of the word. I revised the entire chat we had with him in my head and was sure I was going to mention this in my work.

On our way back, I asked Kartik, "Were you really not convinced? He was great. He made sense. What more did you need to agree? A kick-ass beating?"

"I was trying to get more out of him. He was like a saint, though not the typical one. That's why I could show the audacity to disagree and extract the best of his wisdom.

"Smart, huh!" I patted his back.

"Did you text Upasna? Did you inform her your book is getting published?

I was slightly taken aback with the abrupt mention of her name. "There is hardly any point. She deserves to move on. I don't want to pull her back by thinking of me again."

"Are you still sad about what happened between you and her and how?"

"After the amazing insightful lecture, no! Maybe I wasn't good enough to have her. I am taking it this way."

"I am still telling you, you aren't doing the right thing, man," Kartik said. "Warning is my duty since I am your buddy. Paying heed to my advice is your choice. You must tell her the truth, man. She ought to know the complete story behind your not selling the film rights in your name. Or if not that, at least... At least tell her about the book."

"Chal, ride faster! I have a booking to attend to," I said.

"You won't listen, right?" he said.

"Ride faster!" I dodged.

Kartik and I loaded the luggage on top of the car. He came along with me as it was his rest day from the shop and he had no work to do. There were three giant sized bags that were to be loaded, and required both of us to load them slowly and carefully, one by one. We had picked passengers from Chandigarh International Airport and they were to be dropped in Sector 9A. I hadn't been anywhere near that area since my last visit to Upasna's house.

There were three elderly ladies who wore loose trousers and plain T-Shirts and two middle-aged men in knickers and round hats. They spoke fancy English, particularly the accent. The former occupied the middle seat and the latter took the back one. They seemed pretty disappointed to have come to India. Though they were Indians by origin, which pretty much was apparent from their looks and the Hindi words they used in between, they weren't proud and were constantly comparing.

As we jumped into the car, the lady sitting in between passed me her phone to look at the address. Well, like destiny was out to play me, it was the Sharmas' house that they asked to be dropped at. I looked at Kartik, numb, and he immediately understood the situation. He knew this was going to be tough for me, but I knew from his eyes that he wanted to laugh at destiny's plan. I pressed the gas and headed to the place, wishing I didn't have to face Upasna's family. Since Kartik did not know driving, I couldn't even ask him to take them to the address and excuse myself from the drive.

My heart started to beat faster and currents of fear ran down my spine as we approached the place. Meanwhile, the passengers were talking and enjoying themselves. They had returned to India after many years, it seemed.

"But this wedding, trust me, is going to be very special. After all, she is the last kid in our family to tie the knot. Sharma is going to make his best effort to make this epic," said a female voice in the backseat. It alarmed me.

Kartik looked at me. I almost suffered a heart attack, very sure they were talking of Upasna's marriage. The address was hers, Sharma was her father and she was the youngest in her family among all cousins.

We were no longer together as a couple was one thing, but to learn that I was officially going to lose her, was entirely different. It pained me to the core. The very thought that she was going to live her life with someone else, jerked tears out from my eyes.

"We are just a few minutes away, Chappu," said a female voice, on the last turn to her house. Our face-off was inevitable now, I knew.

I could see the entire Sharma family standing in the distance, looking in our direction. I stopped the car in front of their house. My passengers jumped out of the car like monkeys, to hug their welcoming relatives. Upasna's father, her mother and she herself had noticed me. As expected, they ignored me. I ignored them. I did not have the courage to look into anyone's eyes. They hurriedly took their guests inside.

With my head bowed in embarrassment, Kartik and I unloaded the bags and kept them just at the entrance of the house. By this time, all of them had vanished from the scene. It was only Upasna who stood there watching me. She was repeatedly being called inside by her father, who was shouting her name out. I felt like going and hugging her tight and telling her to not marry someone else or I would be broken.

With the mehndi in her hands and hair tied into a bun, she looked like a dream. My dream. That I had lost.

The entire house had been freshly painted and was decorated with lights. It was hard for me to accept that she was getting married. Kartik nudged me and gestured that I tell her everything. He had forced me to tell her everything after I had left her house the last time. After her father had raised questions on my rationality. I refused to to listen to him. He told me again I wasn't doing justice to her. That she deserved to know. But I was sure he did not understand the gravity of the situation. He did not know how her father's words had perced through my heart. How it had made me want to leave her alone, for her own happiness and bright future. She deserved someone better than me. Tears dropped from Upasna's eyes and it broke my heart. She looked helpless and wounded.

It was having a strange effect on me, but Kartik wasn't left out either. The pain in our eyes made Kartik further get on my nerves.

"Tell her, Bhabhi is crying," he almost shouted in my ear. Upasna's father rushed to her, grabbed her by the arm and took her away. We left too, sad and depressed.

"Once an astrologer told me, your wedding isn't very sure. Might happen, might not happen. But he said one thing with surety – that I will break someone's marriage for sure," Kartik said.

I looked at him sternly. "Dare you do anything weird and I'll chop your head off," I warned him. "Don't create any humiliating situation for anyone, you understand?"

He rubbed his hands, smiling.

"I am warning you, Kartik! This is not a joke; this is someone's life. This is about the dignity of a very reputed family. I am never going to talk to you if you hatch any plot and create nuisance," I said, fuming.

However, I knew well he was notorious. He was surely not going to heed to my warning as he had made up his mind – clear and focused. I wondered if he had to do this sort of non-sense anyway, why he could not do it before! Little did I know he was going to crash in her sangeet ceremony and perform an act of sheer stupidity.

I was unaware of what he was planning, not knowing what evil had already brewed up inside his head. Predominantly, I had ignored the outrageous side of him perceiving he was just acting up, more to irritate or at best instigate me. For the next couple of days, we hardly spoke. I wanted to keep my mind off Upasna and what I had lost in life, and hence was burying myself in work. Whatever he was up to, I was uninformed.

And thankfully, it was also the beginning of the Diwali season. The best time of the year in terms of work. We hardly had a minute free for ourselves. Taxi business in those days in India was on a seasonal flourish. People were travelling, coming home and going out for shopping and other such things, leading to a large number of people travelling.

I was taking advantage of the tide, working day in, day out to earn as much possible. The prime agenda, of course, was to make money to have a smooth investment flow for marketing my soon-to-be released books, and to fulfil my desire of buying a pair of gold bangles for my mother. I knew she never had that before, and had always dreamt of wearing one. Moreover, the better this period (festival period) went, the sweeter would Diwali be for us.

I could vividly recall that my father would be out of sight for many days during this festival period. In order to buy all of us gifts and be able to bring us crackers, he pushed himself into driving for crazy number of hours. However, when I looked back, I realized he had not bought even a pair of slippers for himself on any Diwali. His priority would always be our happiness. Strangely, I never realized that when he was alive. Only when he was gone did I look back and understood the sacrifices he made for his family. I wondered if I was in his place, if I could be half as selfless as he was.

Dropping a few passengers to the Marriot hotel in Chandigarh, I had just arrived back to the railway station taxi stand at around 1:00 a.m. It was mostly empty. I was happy to see a very few taxis, as that increased my probability of getting another customer. I reclined my chair to rest for a bit, deciding to go out on arrival of a train.

I tuned in to the radio and Kishore Kumar's very melodious *Mere sapno ki rani kab aegi tu* was playing. What a delight, I muttered! I loved each and every song by this man as he could invoke the rightest emotion in your heart. I increased the volume a bit, smiling, and thinking that my *sapno ki rani*, the queen of my dreams, had come and gone away. I stretched my body hard and fell back in my chair. Singing along, my eyes closed and yawning, I was trying to catch a short nap. That's when I heard a hard knock on my window.

I looked to my right and I was shocked. No, there wasn't any passenger for a drive or a cop to trouble me for parking my car wrong. It was Upasna Sharma standing in a red *lehenga-choli*. She was dressed as a bride, wearing sparkling red bangles in both her hands. Her hair was left loose in the usual waves that she was always very fond of. But maybe she had cried hard as the kohl in her eyes was all messed up. She looked panic-stricken and continuously knocked against the window, wanting to talk maybe. I quickly opened the door to jump out. She did not give me a moment to utter a word; she put her hand on my chest and pushed me back.

"What happened?" I asked, as she pushed me once more. The back of my knee area hit the car parked behind me, and my hands landed on the bonnet of the car to regain balance. The driver inside the car woke up with the noise and peeked out of the window to see what was going on.

Before I could ask what she was doing and what she was up to, she gave me the tightest slap ever. I kept my hand on my cheek, stunned beyond measure. Bomb-shelled. I could never imagine anything like that from her. As I looked back into her eyes, another slap hit me with equal force on the other side of my face.

"What the...." I almost said, but before I could go on, five or six back to back slaps hit me. It took me half a minute to come out of the impact of what had just happened, and just then, she kicked her knee into my gut. I screamed in pain and fell down on my knees.

The other driver came out of the car, probably thinking that I had misbehaved with this girl and she was hitting me in defense. He stood there watching, because he was happy I was getting beaten up.

Tears were flowing from Upasna's eyes while she screamed, "Fucker! Why did you do this to me? Why?"

I was wondering what the hell she was talking about. What had triggered this reaction, I didn't know. I was holding my crotch and struggling to breathe amidst the excruciating pain.

"I ask you, why? You... you son of a gun, why?" She held me from the collar, making me stand up. Repeating the same question, crying, she hit her hands mightily on my chest. Half her bangles broke, gashing open her skin from a few places.

Her blood trickling down made me freeze. The little air that I was taking in seemed stuck in my lungs. "God, what are you doing?" I tried to stop her.

"What am I doing? And what did you do, you rascal? What did you do to me, huh?" She swept her hand on her face to wipe tears. The way she shouted scared the shit out of me. I was petrified, almost sure she was here to kill me.

"You ruined my life, you moron!" she said, her teeth locked.

"But what on earth did I do?" I asked like a wounded puppy.

"What did you do?" She sarcastically repeated. "What did you do?" She saw here and there on the ground, surely looking for a stick or a stone. At last finding nothing to hit me with, she grabbed me by the collars again.

"I am not sparing you, Paarth Avasthi. This will be the worst night of your life."

"But at least tell me what happened?" I asked.

"If you don't know, I am least interested in revealing." She lifted her hand to slap me again. I closed my eyes tight. Upasna's hand paused. A small crowd of people stood watching us.

"Don't slap me, please. Don't slap me. I am sorry," I begged

She pushed me with both her hands, looked at me for a while and fell on her knees, crying so loud that her wails broke my heart to pieces.

The people in the crowd began to murmur in each other's ears. I wondered, what if they come and hit me, considering I had done something objectionable with Upasna.

I folded my hands before Upasna, reaching down to her. "Can you at least tell me what has happened? Why are you so angry?"

"If I would have gotten married tomorrow, what would you have lost? I was a crazy girl who fell for this driver and he cheated me!" she wailed.

I went near her, "I did not cheat on you. Tell me, please! Why are you crying?"

"You lied to me. Everything was a lie." She hit me again.

"What lie, Upasna?" I almost begged her.

"Everything!" Again a subjective answer amidst loud cries.

I wanted to know what was bothering her; what had led to her being in this state. And I was getting worked up with all the allegations, without being told any reason.

I sat there with my legs folded and told her calmly, "The moment you are done with all this drama, tell me what wrong did I do. I am waiting till then."

She calmed down and said, "You sold your scripts for movies saying your name won't come!"

"Yeah, I did," I said

Her voice went a notch up when she asked, "Then why is my name going to be in the credits?"

Shit, she knew the truth. But how, I wondered.

"Tell me, Paarth!" she repeated.

"Ummm...."

"Paarth, I am asking something."

"Because... that was the real deal, Upasna. No one asked me to leave the stories, take money and not claim ownership. It was in fact I who had requested the producers to put your name in credits as the writer."

"Why did you not tell this to us then? Why did you not tell my father when it meant the most? Why does someone else have to tell me that?"

The tears I had been holding back now came forth in full force. I knew she would know the truth someday, and I could not fathom how to explain to her that her father had said things that had hurt me deeply. It had broken my heart into pieces to learn what he actually perceived of me. He, on such a small mistake, which was not even a mistake, but just half information, said such cruel words! His reaction was so terrible on coming to know that the stories won't be credited in my name, that he gave me a report card on my intelligence and a prophesy on my future. He did not even let me complete what I had to say further.

He had even planned on helping me establish a business when I had clearly told him I wanted to be something else in life. And above all, he was sure I was such a fool that I would squander all his hard-earned money. That is what he really thought of me. However, that, I suppose was good in one way because he wasn't convinced about marrying his daughter to me. Had someday something actually gone wrong, I would have been humiliated by him, and Upasna would have regretted marrying me. That's why I left, knowing I wasn't the right boy for Upasna and her family.

"You are a selfish man, Paarth! The truth is, you did not want to live with me. You could have said that straight. But, no! You cleverly built a ground to leave. You are pathetic. I hate you. I hate you!"

"That's not the truth, Upasna," I finally said.

"That is the only truth, Paarth. Have the guts to admit it! Why would anyone want to be with a worthless girl? You are a big shot writer now. Your books are getting published soon. You are even receiving advances now."

Who on earth told her all that? Kartik?!

"I was about to, actually. I was going to message you." I tried to cover up, "I thought I would surprise you with the first copy."

"Surprise, my foot! After my marriage to someone else, what would have I done seeing your book? Used the pages as toilet paper?"

What the hell is going on in my life?

"Marriage?" I asked her. "You are wearing this because you were..... Umm?"

"I ran away from my sangeet ceremony as soon as I came to know the truth," she said. "You are the one responsible for all this humiliation me and my family are going to suffer now."

"But who told you?" I asked.

"Certainly not you. Because you have no affection left for me."

'Upasna, trust me, I was about..."

"Why did you not then?" she shouted, not letting me finish. "Why? Was your ego more important than my love for you?"

"Don't say that, please," I requested, feeling helpless. How would I have explained my reason of going away.

"Have enough courage to face what you did now."

I did not say anything. I stared down, finally preparing my mind that it was better to explain everything.

I said, "When I came to your home for the meeting, I had a plan. I was going to tell you all I have sold the stories for films, but not in my name, and keep the other part of the news as a small sweet surprise. I had a very strong emotion attached to it. I wanted everyone to know the extent to which I loved you. Maybe I also wanted to convey I can give up for you as much as you could do for me. Nonetheless, before I could go ahead completing what I had to say, your father said things that I knew made sense. They raised questions in my head. I failed to get over the futuristic picture they showed. I didn't want our relationship to seem like a mistake to you someday, and you having to be taunted by your own family in case I ever committed a mistake or ended up ugly."

She was staring at me in disbelief, and then finally let it all out. "Your overthinking got us almost killed. If bad times ever dawned and someone taunted us, I would have stood by you. I would have held you. I fought with my father for you, remember? But you had no faith in me. You didn't know you are the one who matters most to me, not they or what they think."

"Upasna, try to see this from my point of view, please. If I would have made a mistake, a huge mistake, would they not have said the same things? I am not saying he was wrong. I actually stand close on no metric to what you are, to how illustrious your family is. Practically, suppose we failed at establishing peace in the longer run, would you not have blamed yourself for this decision? Tell me!"

"Fuck you… fuck your thoughts. Fuck your perceptions… fuck your existence."

"Please try and understand me, Upasna. Listening to what your father said, I realized no matter how equal and just we may pretend to be, truth remains truth and it comes out."

"No, Paarth. You should have told us all this, then. You should have completed. But you didn't love me enough. You loved your ego more."

"There is nothing I have loved more than you, Upasna. You are my world," I said.

"You don't love me. You have cheated me," she was inconsolable. "Not even once… not for a single time did you try and meet me."

I couldn't look into her eyes anymore. I was torn between right and wrong. On one side was my mind, which knowing how the world worked, connived with my action; while on the other was her love for me which made me feel guilty that I hadn't trusted her enough. Not for a single second in the last half an hour of her shouting at me did her tears stop. I felt I had done a blunder by walking out of her life. She deserved to know the whole truth, but my own apprehensions undid our relationship.

"I was afraid. I felt… I felt your father has no respect for me. Eventually if I didn't have a good career, he would have blamed you for choosing me," I said.

"Keep thinking anything rubbish in your head and hand me over to pain. He also plays with me; you also play with me. Nobody bothered to think of me even once, to ask what I really want!"

"I think of you Upasna… every second, every minute, every hour, eve…."

"No! If that was true, you wouldn't have left me. I have cried for ages. I have cried for every second since you left. You never looked back. You never even asked me how I was. Not even once."

I felt sorry and stupid. Her email had depressed me to an extent and I told her that. She justified herself saying it was a reaction to how her parents had behaved with her when I had left. It wasn't an easy thing to be a girl on some matters where she can emotionally be blackmailed by everyone. She needed my support, she said. On the contrary, I had left to never send her a single message.

"Look into my eyes, do you notice what you mean to me? Tell me, do you notice?" she asked holding my face in rage.

"I do, Upasna," I said.

"So easy it was for you to walk away from my home! There was a girl who had given her soul to you, and you did not think of her even once. She had given all her time

167

to you… and you judged her on the basis of one email she sent. Wow! My father said something, and you said goodbye! Could you not explain what you had actually done? Could you not? Was it so difficult to keep your ego aside, Paarth Avasthi? Did I mean nothing to you?"

"I am sorry."

"Stick this apology up your ass!" she shouted, crying.

How do I calm her down?

"My sangeet ceremony…" She cried more, "You left no stone unturned in sending me to mandap with some… with some… fat ass."

"I am sorry. Please," I requested.

"At this hour, in the dead of the night, I am running around the city to find you, as if I am a lunatic. You are not at your home. Your number is off. You are not with Kartik. I am sure you have something going on with some girl."

I laughed. She was being absolutely childish with her last comment.

"You are selfish. You didn't think of me at all," she added.

"I love you, Upasna. I love you to the moon and back."

"Noooooo, you don't. You don't love me," she said, wiping her tears.

"I swear, honey. I love you."

She got up from the ground. I followed.

"I am sorry. I have said enough. I think I should go back. You are just like other boys. You passed your time with me, and then let me go to hell," she said and turned back.

"You know why I gave your name in the credits, and not mine, Upasna?" I said, calling her back.

"You left a career that could have taken you places. American PR, German PR – we all die for them, isn't it? You left all of that because you wanted a place in my heart." My voice had grown shaky. I was emotional and this was my chance to tell her that I loved her.

She turned back. I was sure she knew I was being honest.

I continued, "For a driver who had no future probably, you made him the most important person of your life. I am sure the world might have told you time and again, giving you a reminder to stop being so stupid. But even once did you let that show in your conduct? No! I never felt I was inferior to you. I never felt I didn't belong to you. You deserve all the credit for making our relationship work... Loving you was very easy for me; I must accept before you. You bettered my life, and yet I failed. Loving me, on the other hand, must have been a challenge for you. You knew you might have to leave everything behind. Isn't it? You were truly an unbelievable gift of god, Upasna. By no means do I want to let you go. I love you."

Upasna walked closer to me. She looked into my wet eyes, keeping her hand on my face. There were tears in her eyes too.

"Why did you not take credit for the stories?" she asked lovingly.

"I wanted to prove to you, your father, your family, the world... that I love you no less. I wanted to show them that if you can quit a career for me, I can match your act of love. Also, I consider you my fortune. The one whose coming into my life made an unexplainable difference. And not that I believe, but I know you have given me a path to follow that brought the best out of me. Otherwise, the new life on the brink of which I stand today, I would never have been thinking of. Recognition wasn't in my wish list. Money has least attracted me. All I have wished for were enough resources to be able to spend my life writing peacefully. So dear lover, I wanted to give the credits of the story to you because you are the reason why all the good happened in my life. I thought, who knows, after this, if I get a chance to show you love or not."

"I love you so much," she said and jumped on me, kissing me deeply. I could feel her soft lips, and all of her flesh on me. Her fragrance was enticing. Our proximity generated a warmth that took my fatigue away. My heart was about to jump out of my chest. As her lips moved around on my lips softly, I felt her passion that exuded immortal love. It sent tremors down my body. I kept my hands on her waist, closing my eyes. I was totally lost and wished this moment never ended. The crowd whistled and the cars honked, but nothing could set us apart.

Upasna's family was overwhelmed to hear my complete story. They knew no one could love their daughter more than I did.

Her father was sorry for what he had said, and I empathized with him. I wanted to forget the past and give life a fresh start. I did not want a feeling of retribution to live inside my heart, as Upasna's father was concerned for his daughter and that was his natural right and responsibility. Any father in the world would have done no different, so I told him it was tough to be in his shoes. He was ecstatic to see my empathy, and expressed joy over the hard work I had put in to make up to his daughter. He even danced with my mother at our wedding. That was fun to watch.

The morning after my marriage, I was in for a grand surprise. Upasna's father got my story published on the front page of all local dailies. It was, he explained to me over the phone, his way of offering an apology. The headlines in the papers read "From a Cabbie to a Film Writer". The news beneath covered everything from how I fell in love with Upasna, the conditions he kept to agree for our relationship to fructify, the efforts I made, credited my stories in her name and everything thereafter.

By the time my second novel released in the market, the extensive coverage in media which I received due to Upasna's father had made me famous already. My book quickly flew off from the shelves like hot cake. The first two editions sold out in the blink of an eye. Of course, the movie was a hit too, and garnered fifteen crores, which was considered a huge amount in Punjabi cinema back then. That undeniably had the biggest role in helping sales of the book across India. Even the first book, which had failed long ago, was republished after its rights were acquired by my publisher of all subsequent books and sold more than a lakh copies within six months.

Most importantly, all my success parties, every single one from when my good times began, Kartik attended them with his girlfriend whom he later married. The most shocking fact was, the girl had approached him. Shaadi.com finally proved to be the saviour as this girl finally agreed to invest her precious life on the worthless him. How on earth was that possible, I always wondered! Anyhow, I played my part trying best to show the girl his real picture. She fell in love with him more each time. I gave up subsequently. His past efforts to have a girl in his life remained the butt of jokes during our get-togethers for a long long time, and I had all plans to share them with his kids. After all, they had every right to know their father's reality. He did not stop calling me 'driver'. That remained my pet name for him even when I only drove for Upasna and my mother and not professionally anymore.

Life was good and had changed completely. I was rich, I had money and I had a good house too. But what stood out for me and what essentially mattered was, I was happy and I felt complete. With that being said, I was sure it was not the end of problems, though. Life was going to bring a fresh set of challenges sooner or later. But till we were together, we could go through any storm and come out holding hands, smiling.

Present Day

You know, it's true love even when years later you care for the other person like nothing else matters anymore. I keep my hands on Upasna's waist as she cleans the make-up with cotton. She carefully rubs it under my eyes and finishing it off, throws the cotton balls in the bin. I know this topic is closed here and she will never reveal it to me how hurt she will remain on not being a mother. I think hard on the solution to save her from this suffering. I understand my presence won't be able to console her, not always. I can be a good redeeming factor at times, no doubt, but looking at women of her age with their kids is surely going to make her feel bad for herself sometimes.

I know what to do. However, I must make it the biggest and the best surprise of her life. To be honest, I have never been a huge fan of adoption for reasons I don't understand. Thinking of it never makes me feel very comfortable. Yes, that sounds stupid, and that's absurd garbage I own in my head, but that's that. You can judge me and tag me with all bad adjectives in the world, but if I don't confess my issues openly to myself and before the world, I won't be able to change ever. And I want to transform.

Having said that, I am going to go in for a two-week counselling session, and by the end of this month, I'll bring an angel daughter who will keep my wife happy. I promise to myself, I'll treat that little one with all the love and affection, and I'll never let her feel she isn't my blood. For she will be an endless source of joy to our family. I'll make sure she has the best father in me, who will love her till the end of time.

I get up from the sofa and before going to change the dress I am wearing, I look into Upasna's eyes and I kiss her.

"I love you, my world! Thank you for being my favourite reason for everything good I do. Thank you so much," I say, holding her tight in my arms.